By Philip Pearce
Illustrated by Darcy Peters

Gypsy Heart Press

Rusti
© 2015 by Philip Pearce

These books are available at special discounts when purchased in quantity for use as premiums, promotions, fundraising and educational use. For inquiries and details, contact: info@gypsyheartpress.com.

Paperback ISBN: 978-0-9969984-0-6
ebook ISBN: 978-0-9969984-1-3
LCCN: 2015918256

Gypsy Heart Press

Navarre, Florida

Chapters

Chapter One

Family

My bedroom door quietly opens.

"Cody, time to get up." Dad's voice rolls across the room, deep and low like distant thunder. He pauses at my door a moment, then his boot-clad footsteps echo on the wood floor as he walks down the hall toward the kitchen.

The scent of brewing coffee drifts into my room. I manage to open one eye and look at the clock. 5:14. Time for us to get up on the farm.

The house feels chilly, just like it does every winter morning. Dad turns the thermostat down when we go to bed at night, and it takes a while for it to warm back up. A body-shaped cocoon of warmth, formed under the goose-down cover where I've been sleeping, envelops me. I inch my foot toward the edge of the cocoon. BRRRRRRR!

It's so cold, almost like sticking my foot in a bucket of ice water. I draw my foot back into the warm cocoon.

Dad's thunderous voice calls, "You awake?"

"Yes, sir," I respond.

"Let's get a move on then. We're burnin' daylight." The floor creaks under his steps as he heads out the back door.

I smile despite my sleepiness. Even though I've heard that expression a thousand times, it still seems funny to imagine sitting around some kind of daylight-fueled campfire.

I've got to get out of bed. With my jaw muscles clenched tight, I sling the covers off in one motion. Whoa, the cold wipes out any lingering sleepiness. I grab a pair of jeans, a flannel shirt, warm socks, and boots, and get dressed as quickly as I can.

As I head for the back door, I hear Mom moving around in Dad's and her bedroom. She's getting dressed and will be starting breakfast soon.

Mom and Dad go well together. They really love each other, and they love us kids. Mom takes care of the house and makes sure it's a great home for our family. Dad takes care of everything outside the house.

Mom's the greatest cook in the whole world. Her pies, cakes, and cobblers are the best. She works as a guidance counselor at a local junior college. Students get advice from her about things like their education, careers, and life. She wants our family to have "a mastery of the social graces." I'm not sure exactly what that means, but I think it's things like chewing food with your mouth closed, brushing your teeth at least twice a day, and always wearing clean underwear.

Dad works as a supervisor in construction. He's more practical. He says everything should have a productive purpose. If it doesn't, he's not that interested in it.

My older sister, Penny, and younger brother, Clay, probably won't get out of bed until the house gets warmer. I like getting up with Dad and doing morning chores. Penny and Clay like some parts of farm life—they especially like going to stock shows with our animals. But, they don't care much for other parts like getting out of bed on a cold morning. I want to be strong and dependable like my dad, willing to get up early and work hard.

At the back door, I put on my hat and coat and then take my flashlight from the shelf above. I go out onto the porch into a shock of icy air that makes inside the house seem almost toasty. A late-March Arctic front has blown through this part of North Texas, and the north wind and frigid temperatures send a shiver from my head all the way down to my toes.

"Yeah, we're burnin' daylight all right," I laugh. "Stars are the only things burnin' at 5:30 in the mornin'. There won't be even a hint of daylight for a while."

The dogs come running with their tails wagging. They bound up and down, making happy high-pitched whimpers. Bobo, our Chow-Labrador mix, is close to ninety pounds and very good-natured. His slick, blondish hair shows the yellow lab part of his breeding. Sancho is a small, funny, terrier mix with a brown scruffy coat that makes him look like he's having a bad hair life.

Simon the cat, a Siamese mix, also waits near the door, not so much because of me but because

he wants to get fed. He has short hair with typical Siamese markings: dark ears, face, tail, and feet. If I behaved like he does, I'd be told that I need an attitude adjustment. He acts like he doesn't care about anybody or anything. He likes me sometimes, but only because he knows I give him fresh milk.

"Hey, you guys. I know you're happy to see me. Glad to see you, too." I greet the dogs with lots of petting and roughhousing, playfully pushing them around and playing little games of tag with them.

They don't understand what I'm saying, but they get all excited and wag their tails when I talk to them anyway. I feed the dogs their breakfast—two big scoops of dog food for Bobo and one scoop for Sancho. Sancho tries to eat from Bobo's dish, but Bobo changes his mind with a low, warning growl. Simon will get his breakfast later.

I grab a clean milk pail and egg basket before I head to the barns then fish around in my coat pockets for my leather gloves so my fingers won't freeze. Simon follows me at a distance, taking a strange, indirect route—typical cat. The dogs will join us after they finish their breakfast.

The three-quarter moon lights the path well enough that I don't need my flashlight. In the trees overhead, two great horned owls hoot back and forth—one nearby and the other farther away. Off in the distance, a coyote pack lets out screaming howls. They remind me that some of the world has been up all night and will soon be going to sleep, while other parts begin to wake up as dawn approaches. This is one of the things I like most about early morning chores.

Chapter Two

Farm

The barns sit about a hundred yards from the house to keep the smell of manure from invading the house during rainy weather. At the barns, I find Dad carrying two five-gallon buckets of water to fill the animals' watering troughs. When the weather is warmer, we fill the troughs using hoses attached to a bunch of nearby faucets, but in this kind of weather, it isn't worth the risk of having exposed faucets freeze and burst. It's hard work to use only the one protected faucet and carry the water to the troughs, but it's better than repairing and replacing water lines and faucets.

Dad's a very strong man. He fills the two buckets and carries them like they're full of feathers instead of water. When I carry one bucket filled about three-fourths the way full, I struggle, bang the bucket against my legs, and slosh some of the water out on the way. For being thirteen years old, I'm fairly strong. But, my hope is, if I keep working at it, I'll be as strong as Dad someday.

Normally my first chore is to feed our 4-H pigs and lambs, which we raise to show at livestock shows and fairs. Since we've just finished with the spring shows, all our show animals have either been sold or brought home to the farm for breeding stock.

Now a new crop of pigs is being farrowed for shows this coming fall. I feed the four sows that are housed in the farrowing houses with their new litters. All the sows and baby pigs look good and healthy. Their tummies are full, their hair is slick and shiny, and they're active and playful. While the mama sows are eating breakfast, their babies are piled up like link sausages, sleeping under heat lamps to keep warm. The pigs on top of the piles are shivering anyway on this frosty morning.

"'Bout time for that old red sow?" Dad mentions a particular sow ready to farrow as he finishes up his part of morning chores.

"Yes, sir. I'll get her in a farrowin' house this evenin'. Not lookin' forward to the fight though."

I continue feeding the pigs and then move to the chickens and our steer. We don't feed our pigs kitchen scraps or anything like that. As Dad tells it, "We feed all our animals scientifically formulated rations that maximize health, growth, and development, and are safe for consumers. Our chickens get a diet that helps them lay high-quality, good-tasting eggs." The steer we're feeding now will put beef in our freezer later.

The pigs whine and grunt loudly until I pour feed in their troughs. The chickens get off their roosts and make sharp clucking sounds until their troughs are filled. The steer makes a sad-sounding *moo* while waiting for his feed. If they could talk, they would probably be saying, "Will you hurry and get me my food," or "Why did you feed other animals before me?"

I reassure them that I'm going as fast as I can, but they can't understand what I'm saying. They also don't care. They just want to be fed. When several pigs share a pen, they fuss at each other about not getting a fair share of the feed even after they've eaten.

After all the animals are fed, I gather eggs. Some of the hens are out in the yard eating from the troughs, while others are still nice and cozy on their nests. The ones on the nests peck at my fingers when I reach under them to retrieve their warm eggs.

I save milking our Jersey cow for last. Since we have only one milking cow, we don't need to spend money on a milking machine. Instead, I just milk her by hand. Before I start, I have to wash her udder. That way, anything she might have been lying on during the night won't fall in the milk pail. This means getting my hands and the cow's udder wet, something neither of us enjoys on a frosty morning.

In the milking shed, we're protected from the wind, which helps some. The cow's udder also provides me with a little warmth while I'm milking. I put my head and shoulder against the cow's side and begin milking her. Soon I get into a rhythmic cadence as I squeeze milk from her udder. *Splosh, splosh, splosh, splosh.* The streams of milk squirt into the pail.

Simon and Sancho sit nearby, watching intently while I'm milking. Without missing a beat, I direct a stream of milk at Simon. *Zap*, right in his face. He jumps straight up in the air, but then quickly settles back in his spot, wiping the milk with his paw and licking if off. *Zap*, I get a direct hit on Sancho's nose. He flicks his head up and down, right and left, looking all around. I zap them several more times. We do this same routine every morning, but both animals seem surprised when they get squirted. They make me laugh so hard that I almost forget I'm supposed to be milking the cow.

The cow brings my attention back to her when she flicks me with her mud-and-manure-caked tail. "Ouch! C'mon, girl. That hurts." Getting slapped across the face with that disgusting thing sort of feels like being swatted by a thorn bush. It would hurt any time, but it's even more painful since my cheeks are cold. Using the back of my hand, I try to rub the sting away.

After I finish the milking, I pour Simon a dish of fresh milk for his breakfast. He acts much friendlier when I feed him. He purrs and rubs on my leg, almost as if he likes me.

Then I head back to the house with the eggs and milk. I can tell all the animals are happy now that their bellies are full. Their restlessness has been replaced by sounds of contentment, and while some are still browsing around, most are settling down for an after-breakfast nap. The sows in the farrowing houses are lying down, letting their baby pigs nurse. I love knowing that they're happy and relaxed. It's another thing I really like about doing morning chores.

Chapter Three

School Time

"Aw, that smells so good!" I exclaim as I push the back door closed with my foot. "I'm flat-out starved!"

The scent of coffee now mixes with the mouth-watering smells of breakfast. It's around 6:30 when I get back to the house, and the glow of dawn lights up the eastern horizon. It's much warmer in the house now than when I left an hour ago.

Mom takes the milk and eggs from me, and I dash to my room to change from smelly work clothes into school clothes. I wash up and hurry to the kitchen for breakfast. We're having pork sausage patties, scrambled eggs, cream gravy, and homemade biscuits with apricot jelly. It doesn't get much better than this. I pour myself a tall glass of milk. After doing morning chores, a big hot breakfast tastes awesome.

Dad's eaten his breakfast and gone to work. Penny helped Mom with breakfast and made sack lunches for everyone, and now she's back in her room doing whatever it is teenage girls do that takes them so long to get ready. Mom's in and out of the kitchen, finishing breakfast and taking care of the fresh milk. Clay's still sitting at the table, using his fork to draw designs in the gravy left on his plate. He's not much into the day-to-day stuff of working on a farm, so he often doesn't help with morning chores. Besides, he'd probably complain the whole time, which would really make it a drag for everyone else.

Neither Clay nor Penny like farm life as much as I do, but that's okay. Mom says we should all find what we enjoy doing, then work hard to do our very best at it. Clay loves sports. He reads everything he can about sports, and he knows ridiculous amounts of facts about football and baseball players. He's taller than all the other kids in his grade at school, and he's faster and more coordinated than a lot of kids who are older than him. Dad says it's too early to tell if he's athletically gifted or if he's just developing more quickly than the other kids.

With help from Mom, Penny is becoming a good cook and can sew some of her own clothes. In school, she really does well in science. Mom says she thinks she'll have a career in medicine.

Clay is four years younger than me, but Penny and I are only eighteen months apart. She and I fuss at each other like a lot of brothers and sisters do, but I'm really glad she's my sister. Nobody else better pick on her, or they'll have to answer to me.

I'm not so great at sports. I'm about average height for my age and not that fast. When they timed us in Phys. Ed. to see how fast we could run, I think they used a calendar for me instead of a stopwatch.

What I love is working on the farm. It's hard work, but in the end, I feel like I've really done something. My favorite parts are trying to figure out which animals might win in the show ring and watching them grow and develop. In the last year or so, I've gotten interested in some of the more technical things, like how many pounds of

feed it takes for a pig to gain a pound of body weight. In school, I do well in math. Dad says I'm very good at problem solving on the farm. Mom thinks I'll be an engineer, which is fine with me as long as I can continue to be around farming and raising animals.

After breakfast, I grab a sack lunch and stuff it in my backpack, then hurry to the bathroom to brush my teeth before the school bus arrives. I haven't quite finished with my teeth when I hear Bobo's distinctive bark—which kind of sounds like it's echoing off a canyon wall. Bobo and Sancho hear the school bus before they see it, so they stand in the front yard barking to let everyone know it's almost here. Simon's probably watching from the porch and yawning. It's funny how he stays close to the action even when he tries to act like he doesn't care.

Penny, Clay, and I grab our backpacks, tell Mom we love her and give her a kiss, and then bolt out the door. We have a daily race to see who can get to the bus stop first.

The dogs know when the school bus brings us home in the afternoon, too. When we get there,

Bobo and Sancho are standing in the front yard to give us a warm welcome by barking and wagging their tails. Simon sleeps in his spot on the porch.

I change back into work clothes and head to the barns to feed and water the animals.

but not without her moaning and groaning the whole time. I run over to the valve box and open the valve that feeds water to the wash rack. When I get back, I rinse the sow off and fill a bucket with soapy water.

I can bathe most of our sows without getting myself all wet. With this sow, that ain't happenin'. It's chilly, and she doesn't like getting wet any more than I do. The soapy water gathers in her coarse, red hair. She shakes often, and I get splattered with it. The longer I scrub her, the wetter I get. The chill settles into my clothes and I begin to shiver. By the time I finish giving the sow a bath, I'm soaked, freezing, and ready to be done with this grouchy old mama.

While she's still in the wash rack, I get some towels to dry her. I don't want her to stay wet any longer than she has to. It's not worth the risk of her getting sick and losing her babies. Her coarse hair jabs me, like pins and needles, while I'm drying her. I run back and close the water valve before taking her out of the wash rack.

When I open the wash rack gate to let the sow out, she stubbornly locks her feet down and refuses to come out.

I laugh in spite of it all. "Are you kiddin' me? Now you like it in there?" I ask. "You're about as sharp as a marble." I have to push her out, and then while I'm driving her to the farrowing house, she tries to double back to the wash rack—the same place she fought going into a few minutes ago!

I finally get her into the farrowing house and feed and water her. This helps her calm down. With all the trouble she gives us, it's a good thing she raises good show pigs that place at the top of their classes at stock shows and bring premium prices when we sell them.

Having finished the rest of my afternoon chores, I return to the house to eat supper, do my homework, and get dry and warm. Before I go to bed I have some time to watch TV and play games with Clay and Penny. But after a long day, I'm ready to crawl into my nice, warm bed a little earlier than usual.

Chapter Five

New Litter of Red Pigs

During farrowing season, I check a sow every three to four hours, except when I'm at school, to see if she's started having her pigs. When I have to check her during the night, I sleep in my clothes so I can get to the barns quickly. If she hasn't started farrowing, I can get back to bed sooner.

At 11:00 on Friday night, I go out to check the sow again. She has made a "nest" by gathering together all the straw bedding in the farrowing house, and she's lying in it. Milk droplets are forming on her nipples, which means she's about to start having her babies. I get right in the farrowing house with her.

When baby pigs are first born, they're covered with slick, slimy stuff. Dad has taught me that it's not good for them to stay wet too long, especially in frigid weather, because they might get too cold and die. We keep a stack of soft, dry towels in one of the barns, which I use to dry off the newborn pigs to warm them up as much as possible. Once their mouths and noses are clear so they can breathe, I try to help each baby learn to nurse. I pry its mouth open, put one of the sow's nipples into its mouth, and squeeze in some milk. Some pigs figure out how to nurse right away, while others need a little more time.

"Hey, cut it out you ol' grouch," I say as the old sow chases me out of the farrowing house. "I'm not gonna hurt your babies. Just let me help."

She doesn't understand what I'm saying, but it wouldn't really matter if she did. It's her job to protect her new babies from anything she thinks might harm them, and she takes her job seriously. She chases me out of the farrowing house three times, while she's giving birth to her pigs.

I wait outside until she settles down, then creep back in as quietly as possible and continue to help deliver her babies. They come along almost like clockwork, one about every fifteen minutes.

By now it's the middle of the night and I'm sleepy. It seems like I yawn with almost every other breath. The pig I just delivered went smoothly. I dried it off and it started nursing with very little help from me. Since I have a break between pigs, I climb out of the farrowing house to try to wake up and warm up some.

I try to think of a song I can sing and dance around to. I look up at the sky, and the only thing I can think of is "Twinkle, Twinkle, Little Star." It's not easy to bust a good dance move to "Up above the world so high/Like a diamond in the sky," but I give it my best shot and then laugh out loud. I'm glad nobody's around to video me.

After a few minutes, I slip back into the farrowing house. I'm awake now, but I might have a worse problem than being sleepy. I now have "Twinkle, Twinkle, Little Star" stuck in my head. I'm afraid I'll be singing it the rest of the night. "C'mon, sow. Gimme another pig," I tell her. "Gotta get that song out of my head."

A few minutes later, she bails me out.

Newborn pigs are cute as can be. They're only a little bigger than a hot dog, and their little faces and feet make them look more like toys than animals. They try to grunt like their mama, but their grunts are so high pitched that they make me laugh. When they're first born, they stumble around, but they'll learn to walk, run, and play like the older pigs in only a few hours.

The sow gives birth to nine healthy pigs, all solid red. I've finished delivering the litter, and they've all nursed. Once their little bellies are full of milk, I help them get under the heat lamp to rest. Being born takes a lot of their energy.

It's 2:30 in the morning when I get back to the house and into bed. Getting up in the middle of the night and delivering a litter of pigs is hard work, especially when it's as chilly as it's been these last few days. Now that I'm in bed, I realize how tired I am, but to know I helped bring a fine litter of healthy pigs into the world makes me feel great. It's another one of my favorite things about living on a farm.

Chapter Six

The Sow Gets Injured

What's goin' on with these babies? I wonder as I feed the red sow and check on her litter. Everything had been going well since they were farrowed. She had recovered from giving birth, and the pigs had been nursing well and were starting to grow. That is, until the Friday after they were born. I notice that the little pigs are now looking a bit ragged—weak and hungry.

I check out the sow and realize she has a swollen, raw spot on one of her nipples. Something obviously injured her, and when I look around the farrowing house for what could've happened, I notice a rusty nail has worked its way out of a board. The sow must have laid on the nail. I pull the nail out of the board to make sure it doesn't hurt her again—or one of her babies.

By the time a pig is about a week old, it wants to nurse from the same spot on its mama every time. One of the babies, a pretty little gilt, a female, keeps trying to nurse on the sore nipple, and that's causing a problem. When the little pig tries to nurse, it hurts the sow. She stands up, and then none of the pigs get to nurse very much. It's no wonder they're looking thin.

"Dad, the ol' red sow injured herself on a nail in one of the boards," I tell him as we feed the animals that evening. "It looks bad. It must hurt her a lot when a pig tries to nurse, because she gets right up."

Dad looks it over and agrees with me. "I'll start doctorin' her, but it'll take at least a week to heal. If the pigs don't get to nurse much while the sow's healin', they'll keep gettin' weaker. Some might even die." Dad sighs and says, "I don't ever like to do it, but the pig tryin' to nurse the injured nipple will need to be put down. If we don't, we might lose the whole lot of 'em. We'd lose that little one anyway."

I know Dad's right, but I don't want the little gilt to be put down. I say, "Instead of puttin' the

pig down, what if I take her to the house and try to bottle-feed and hand-raise her? We've raised some that way in the past and it's worked out okay."

Dad scratches his head as he thinks it over. "We have had luck doin' that, but I don't much like to hand-raise animals. Carin' for 'em that way can take up a lotta time, and that's time that might be needed for doin' other chores and carin' for other animals. That said, I've noticed that you take a lot of responsibility for gettin' your chores done and keepin' up with your schoolwork, so I'll think about makin' an exception in this case."

After more thought, he says, "If I let you try to bottle-feed the little gilt, you'll have to agree to some rules. First, you'll have to continue to do all your other chores. Second, you'll have to keep up with your schoolwork. Your grades can't go down because of the time you spend takin' care of that pig. And third, when the other pigs in her litter are weaned, she'll have to go back to live with 'em. Do we have a deal?"

"Oh yes, sir," I tell him. "It's a deal."

Dad nods at me. "I'm countin' on you, Cody. Don't let me down."

I know I won't.

Chapter Seven

Preparing a New Home

It's Saturday, and I'm excited to spend some time getting things ready to care for the little gilt. After Dad and I finish our morning chores, we look for a place where she can live. She'll need a spot that's protected from the cold and big enough to provide room for her as she grows. I'm hoping we can find someplace nearer to the house than the barns so I can keep a close watch on her.

"What if we put her in the storage shed near the house?" Dad suggests as we walk together from the barns to the house. "There's a soft dirt floor that'll be good for her feet. We only use it to store tools and tractor parts anyway."

We head to the storage shed, where Dad and I move stuff around to make room for a small pen. I build a pen out of wire panels and put down fresh straw for bedding.

When in the litter, baby pigs huddle close together to stay warm, but this little gilt will be alone in her pen. Since the nights are still chilly, I hang a heat lamp in one corner of her pen. She'll keep warm sleeping under it. When we're finished, the pen in the shed looks like it'll make a great new home for the young pig.

Chapter Eight

Time for the Move

Now it's time to move the gilt to her new pen. It won't be easy to take one of the Duroc sow's pigs away from her, so we make a plan to catch and remove the little gilt. We hope it will work without the sow catching either of us in the process.

Dad lays out the plan: "Cody, you get on one side of the farrowing house and I'll get on the other. When I distract the sow, you grab the gilt and lift her over the fence."

We make our first attempt. Dad makes some noise from his side of the pen, and, as planned, the sow goes over to see what he's doing. I reach down and grab the gilt's foot, but it slips in my hand. I have a hold only on her toes, so I can't lift her over the fence. The pig squeals, and the sow charges to my side of the farrowing house to protect her baby. The sow chomps her teeth, grunting loudly, and I have to turn loose of the little gilt.

Bobo and Sancho hear the commotion and decide to add their voices to the ruckus, barking and howling. Even sows in nearby farrowing houses start making angry grunting noises.

"Cody, watch that ol' sow!" Dad yells. "She'll bite you if she gets half a chance."

The sow wheels around and makes a hard run at Dad. He is straddling the fence, and when he sees the sow steaming full speed in his direction, he quickly pulls his foot out of the pen and over the fence.

I can't keep from laughing out loud. "You'd better watch her yourself," I say. "She had you right in her sights that time."

"I'll bang on a feed bucket," Dad calls to me over all the noise. "Maybe that'll distract her enough for you to catch the pig."

By now, the sow is focused on me. The feed bucket doesn't distract her at all. Her instinct is to protect her babies, and she isn't interested in eating.

Dad reaches over the fence and grabs one of the other pigs by the leg as it runs by him. It lets out a deafening squeal, and the sow wheels around and goes charging after Dad again. I jump over the fence into the farrowing house, race over to the pigs huddled in a corner of the pen, and grab the gilt. As soon as I pick her up, she lets out her own ear-piercing squeal. Knowing how the sow is going to respond, I hightail it back the way I came, cradling the pig securely in my arms.

"Run, Cody!" yells Dad. "She's right on your tail."

But I don't need Dad to tell me what she's doing. I can almost feel her hot breath on my leg. "C'mon, feet. Don't fail me now!" I hear her teeth chomping at me only inches away. When I get to the fence, I bail over it in one motion, landing safely away from the sow on the other side. "Phew! That was close," I tell Dad. "Thought she was gonna get me."

Even after I get her out of the pen, the gilt squeals so loudly that I'm sure the neighbors can hear her. The poor thing's little heart is pounding hard against my fingers, which are wrapped

around her chest. The sow stands at the fence, still chomping her teeth, grunting, and acting like she might try to come over the fence after me. Bobo and Sancho continue to bark and howl and jump around. The whole thing makes for a loud and chaotic chorus. I wrap the little pig in a burlap sack to help calm her down, and Dad and I take her to her new pen.

"Might be a good idea if you don't tell your mom how close that old sow got to you," Dad says as we're walking toward the house. "No use gettin' somethin' stirred up with her."

I grin and nod in agreement. Some stories are better left at the barns.

At first, the gilt doesn't like her new pen at all. She's all by herself, and she misses her mama and littermates. She runs around the pen, squealing and grunting. I get some powdered milk, mix it with water in a bottle, and give it a good shake. Then I sit down in the pen with her to try to feed her.

"I know it doesn't seem like it right now, but I think you'll like it here once you get used to it," I tell the young pig. "And you can bet you'll be healthier."

She finally takes to nursing from the bottle. She's so hungry that she almost pulls it out of my hand. It's the most milk she's had to drink for a day or more. The cute way she wrings her tail as she sucks the milk from the bottle makes me laugh. She settles down and starts looking more comfortable.

From outside the pen, Bobo and Sancho watch what's going on and wag their tails. Simon, high on a shelf overlooking the pen, pretends to have no interest in the morning's events. After the little gilt finishes the entire bottle of milk, she stretches out under the heat lamp for a well-deserved nap.

While she's sleeping, I slip back to the farrowing house to see how her mama and the rest of her littermates are doing. The sow is calmer, lying down letting her pigs nurse. She grunts rhythmically, almost like she's singing a lullaby to her babies. They're already starting to look healthier after getting this one good meal in their bellies. So far, our plan to save the litter seems to be working just the way Dad and I hoped it would.

Chapter Nine

A Name for the Little Gilt

"Don't you think this little gilt should have a name?" I ask Dad as we check on the pig we've rescued. "We can't just keep calling her *little gilt*." I think back to the rusty old nail that caused her mama's injury. That's why she's living here in the shed now. Her red hair sort of reminds me of the color of that rusty nail, so I say, "What if I name her Rusty but spell it like a girl's name: R-U-S-T-I?"

"You know I don't much like to give the animals names," Dad responds. "We're not raisin' pets here. You get too attached to animals when you start namin' 'em. It can make it harder to do what needs to be done when the time comes— when we have to sell 'em or use 'em for food."

"I know. And I'll try not to get too attached

to her." Deep down, though, I know that'll be difficult.

Rusti is cute as a button. Her hair color is kind of auburn rather than light red, like a lot of pigs of her breed. She has long, dark eyelashes, and it almost looks like she's wearing eye makeup. With dark eyes and a somewhat short snout, her face has a charming expression that makes it seem like she understands when I talk to her. The hair on the tuft of her tail is a little darker than the rest of her, which makes it even more noticeable when she wrings her tail. I decide Rusti is the cutest little pig I've ever seen.

Chapter Ten

Keeping Rusti Healthy

How can I make sure Rusti gets the nutrition she needs when I'm not here? I wonder as I feed her again that afternoon. Baby pigs, like all babies, need to eat many times a day. Their little bellies don't have a lot of room, so they nurse a lot to get all the nutrients they need to grow. During the day, I'll be at school and Mom and Dad will be working, so no one will be home to feed her.

Watching her little tail curl, I get an idea. *If I build a bottle holder, I can hang a bottle of milk in the pen.* That way Rusti can drink it while everyone's gone. That afternoon, I set about building a bottle holder that I think might work.

After Rusti finishes her last bottle of milk for the night, I mix another one to hang in the bottle holder. I put it near the heat lamp, hoping the lamp will keep the milk a little warmer in the cold night air. The next morning I check to see if Rusti has drunk the milk from the bottle in the holder during the night. She hasn't touched it, but she's obviously very hungry. Her noisy grunts and squeals let everyone know how upset she is.

After mixing a fresh bottle of milk, I start feeding it to Rusti. She drinks a few gulps, and then I pull the bottle away from her mouth and move it a little closer to the holder. Then I let her start drinking again. I repeat this trick a couple more times before hanging the bottle in the bottle holder. This time, Rusti starts drinking milk from the bottle in the holder, wringing her little tail as she does. I go on to the barns to do my chores while she finishes her breakfast.

When I've done my chores, I go back to the house to get dressed to go to church with my family. Before we leave, I run out to Rusti's pen, mix another bottle of milk, and hang it in the bottle holder. I want to see if she'll drink the milk while we're gone.

I'm anxious to get home from church and check on Rusti. As soon as the car stops moving, I jump out, hurry inside to change into my

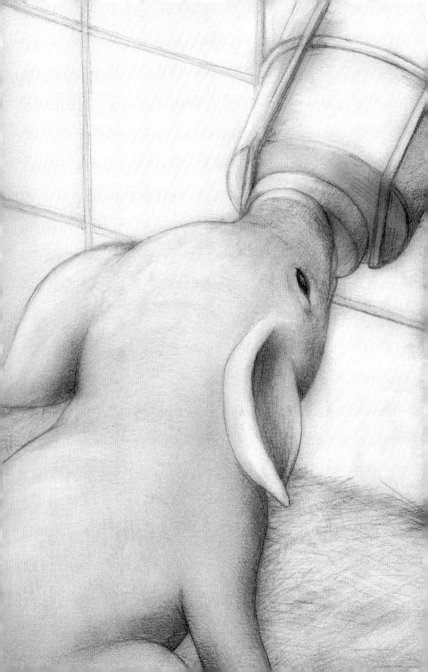

work clothes, and run to her pen. There, I find her sleeping peacefully under the heat lamp while Bobo, Sancho, and Simon keep watch over her. The bottle in the holder is empty.

I smile and say to the dogs, "No reason this won't work just as well while I'm at school."

On Monday morning after I finish my chores, I find an extra-large bottle. I mix Rusti some milk and hang it in the bottle holder before I catch the school bus. When I get off the bus in the afternoon, I run out to check on Rusti. She's drunk all the milk from the bottle during the day. Now she's hungry again, but she's healthy.

This makes me proud. The bottle holder worked like a charm. "We're gonna make this hand-raisin' thing work, Miss Rusti, and you're gonna grow into a fine pig," I say to her as I mix another bottle of milk. I think about giving her a high-five, but pigs aren't that great at taking high-fives. I settle for giving her a rub behind her ears instead.

Settling into a routine, I take care of Rusti along with my other chores and schoolwork. In the evenings after I eat supper and finish my homework,

I go out to her pen and clean up poop and any-thing else, so her pen doesn't start to stink. Then I add fresh straw and sit with her for a while.

Most pigs are curious about people but don't like to get too friendly or allow too much contact. Because I'm kind of a substitute mom for Rusti, she doesn't seem to mind being close to me. Plus, she's a lot more curious than most little pigs. She likes to crawl in my lap and nuzzle me with her snout. I laugh and scratch her tummy and rub behind her ears, which she seems to like a lot. She stands there wringing her little tail.

Sometimes, I leave her gate open and Bobo and Sancho come into the pen to snuggle with Rusti and me. Simon wants to join in, but that would be getting too friendly for his taste, so he sits on the high shelf pretending to be sleeping or keeping watch on some imaginary insect.

A few mornings later, Mom makes oatmeal for breakfast. I get back from doing my chores a little later than usual, so I'm the last one to eat. After I finish, at least one serving of oatmeal is left over. "You think it'd be okay if I take the rest of the oat-meal to Rusti?" I ask Mom as she's cleaning up the kitchen. "I wanna see if she'll eat it with some of her milk on it."

"Well, leftover oatmeal isn't much good for anything," Mom replies. "I'd likely throw it out, so you can take it to her."

When giving the oatmeal to Rusti, I tell her, "Eatin' this'll be different than drinkin' from a bottle. Give it a try. You might like it."

Rusti is interested in the oatmeal from the start, but eating solid food is a lot different for her. With small bites at first, she begins to get the hang of it.

From then on, I ask Mom to fix oatmeal for breakfast and make some extra for Rusti. Oatmeal is a fast and easy option for breakfast when Mom's in a hurry. Most days she likes to make a farm-type breakfast like bacon and eggs with biscuits and gravy, but she decides she can make oatmeal for Rusti and me.

Rusti regularly gets leftover oatmeal, and I start to bring pig feed from the barns for her. Soon she'll be weaned from milk, so she needs to get used to eating regular feed. She's growing into a fine, healthy young pig.

Chapter Eleven

Rusti Becomes a Yard Pig

The school year is now winding down and summer's coming. It stays light longer into the evening, and I often let Rusti out of her pen to get some exercise in the yard.

For the first few days when I let her out, she and I play in the yard by ourselves. But after a while, Bobo and Sancho join in on the fun. Soon I get left out, with Rusti, Bobo, and Sancho playing a game of tag. Rusti and Sancho tear around chasing after Bobo, scurrying along as fast as their short legs will carry them. Bobo's longer legs and bigger body allow him to dodge the two smaller animals' attempts to catch him and knock him down.

When Rusti and Sancho try to make sharp turns to catch Bobo, they often lose their balance,

roll over several times, and end up sprawled in the grass. If they do catch him, they pounce on him and wallow around with him. My whole family laughs out loud as we watch their games of tag.

Simon sits on a tree stump a few feet out of the line of attack, keeping a close watch on the games, while trying to come across as being above all of their nonsense. He looks down his nose at them—that is, when he bothers to look at them at all. He often pretends to be asleep. After they play for a while, I lead Rusti back into her pen and close and latch her gate.

Late one night, just as I'm falling asleep, I jolt awake with a terrible thought. I can't remember latching Rusti's gate when I put her in her pen. I jump out of bed in a panic. My mouth is dry, my heart pounds in my chest, and I feel sweat gathering on my forehead. I quietly creep out of the house, then dash out to the storage shed.

Her gate is open and she's not in her pen. I feel sick to my stomach, like I may throw up. *What if something's happened to Rusti? What if she's wandered away, become lost, and can't find her way home? What if she's gotten out on the road and been run over by a car?* I imagine a long list of terrible things that could happen to her.

Grabbing my flashlight, I hurry into the yard and frantically search all around in desperate hope that she may not have wandered far. I look under every bush, around Mom's car and Dad's truck, behind trees, and as far down the path to the barns as the beam from my flashlight will reach.

Finally, I go over near the porch where Bobo and Sancho sleep, hoping maybe they'll help me find her. In the pale moonlight, I see Bobo and Sancho asleep, and there's Rusti lying with her head against Bobo's chest—safe and sound! Relief washes over me.

Bobo stirs slightly when he hears me. He raises his head and looks at me as if to say, "No worries. We've got this."

"You're a good dog, Bobo," I say in a low voice.

He slaps his tail on the ground several times then lays his head back down.

I go back to bed very relieved. My heartbeat is almost back to normal, and I can finally make enough saliva that I can swallow. Wow, was that ever a close call!

When I go out the back door on my way to the barns in the morning, Bobo, Sancho, and Rusti are waiting in the yard. Because she seems to be content to stay in the yard, I decide to let her stay out of her pen most of the time, except while I'm at school.

Chapter Twelve

Market Gardening

"Cody, you need to make sure the fence around the garden is Rusti-proof," Dad says one morning as we pass the garden on the way to the barns. "It won't be good for her to get in there and start rootin' around. Even as little as she is, you know how much she can tear things up. Besides, if she ever gets started, it'll be hard to keep her out."

Last year, several pigs got out of their pen and wandered into our garden. Boy, did they ever make a mess of it. They ate some of the vegetables and destroyed a lot more by rooting, playing, and tearing everything up. We had just watered it that morning, so it looked like the pigs had a mud-wrestling party. It took us most of two weeks to clean everything up, re-plow the rows, and replant. The produce from the garden

wasn't ready to be picked until almost a month later than it should have been because of those *destructo* pigs.

In addition to growing fruits and vegetables for our family to eat, we raise extra produce to sell to the local grocer and at our own produce stand. With meat, milk, eggs, and the fruits and vegetables from the garden, we raise much of the food we eat. And because it's all so fresh, it's very healthy for us.

There's always something to do in the garden. We prepare the soil and do the planting. We water about every other day unless it rains. The plants need to be fertilized now and then. Then there's produce to be gathered. The worst job is weeding. Pig weed and thistles seem to spring up a foot tall overnight. They can get out of control if we don't keep them pulled or hoed. It seems like I can pull or hoe weeds all day every day and still not be able to keep up with them.

Penny, Clay, and I operate a small roadside produce stand near the highway in front of the house. Dad says he's not all that worried about running a profitable business. He mostly wants us kids to learn to be responsible. We tend the garden and pick, wash, and market the produce. In exchange, we're rewarded with spending money that we can use to buy a burger or go to a movie. That is, as long as I make sure the fences around the garden are in good shape so Rusti or any *destructo* critters can't get in there and tear it up.

Chapter Thirteen

The Escape Artist/ School Bus Greeter

Rusti's now a little more than three weeks old. She no longer drinks milk and is healthy and growing by eating leftover oatmeal and pig feed. Her littermates have also been weaned from nursing the red sow.

"You remember we agreed that Rusti'll return to live with her littermates when they're weaned?" Dad reminds me one evening while we're feeding the animals.

I remember. As much as I want to keep her to myself, Dad's taught me how important it is to do what I say I'll do. My commitment doesn't change even when circumstances change. "I wish I didn't have to take Rusti to live with the other pigs," I say as I throw dirt clods at an old bucket hanging on a fence post. "They probably won't remember her, and she'll be livin' in a strange place. But that's what I agreed to do, so I'll do it."

"I'm proud of you for being a man of your word," Dad tells me. "That's integrity. It'll serve you well as you get older."

So Bobo, Sancho, Simon, and I make the long, difficult walk to the barns with Rusti.

When I put her in the pen with her littermates, they have forgotten her. It's obvious they don't like her. Two of the larger pigs are especially mean. They seem to lead the other pigs in mistreating Rusti, biting at her and chasing her around the pen. They won't even let her lie under the shed with all the other pigs, and they run her off every time she tries to eat at the feed trough. Pigs try to use the bathroom as far away from their food, water, and sleeping place as possible. The two mean pigs won't let Rusti lie anywhere but in a corner of the pen near where the pigs go to poop.

"Don't worry too much about her," Dad says. "Those pigs'll all get used to each other after a while. They'll be fine."

Reluctantly, I leave Rusti in the pen with the other pigs.

When it's time to go back to the house, Bobo and I lag behind to see if things are any better for Rusti. The two lead pigs go to where Rusti's lying to chase her around some more, biting at her and rooting her around with their snouts. When Bobo sees what they're doing, the hair on his neck and back bristles up. He jumps the fence into the pen with the pigs and gets between the two mean pigs and Rusti. He lets out three loud barks followed by a low growl.

Pigs and dogs don't speak the same language, but the two pigs obviously have no problem understanding Bobo. It's almost like he's saying, "You want to pick on my friend? You'll have to go through me first." The pigs back off and go lie with the other pigs under the shed.

Satisfied that they aren't going to pick on Rusti for the time being, Bobo jumps back out of the pen. He and I start toward the house. "You're a good dog, Bobo," I tell him as I pat his head.

He wags his tail in appreciation of the praise.

Rusti makes loud squealing and grunting noises after us, sounding sadder and more miserable than I've ever heard her.

Bobo and I take a few steps, stop to look back at her, and then look at each other. We feel like we're deserting our friend.

"She sure doesn't want to stay with those other pigs, and I can't say as I blame her," I tell Bobo. "Especially those two mean pigs. She wants to live in the yard with you guys."

But I know she needs to stay where she is, so Bobo and I trudge back to the house without her.

The next morning when I head out the back door to do my chores, Rusti is right there in the yard with Bobo and Sancho, waiting to be fed. After I finish my chores, I go to the pen where I left her the night before. She's pushed a small hole in the fence and crawled out. I repair the fence and put Rusti back in the pen before the school bus arrives. "You've gotta stay here," I tell her. "You might even learn to like it." But even I'm not so sure about that.

That afternoon, Bobo and Sancho are in the yard, waiting for the school bus as usual. They're barking and wagging their tails, welcoming the three of us home. Right beside them is Rusti, grunting as loud as she can and wringing her tail, which makes it look like she's wagging it.

When Clay, Penny, and I get off the school bus, we can clearly see the faces of all the other kids pressed against the windows. They're pointing, laughing, and yelling things like, "Look, that little pig thinks it's a dog," "Cody has a pig that tries to bark and wag its tail," and "I guess their family has a watch pig." Clay and I think it's hilarious, but Penny isn't at all amused.

After my evening chores, I repair the fence again and return Rusti to the pen with the other pigs. When I go out to check on her after eating supper and doing homework, I find Rusti has broken out of the pen again and is back in the yard with Bobo and Sancho. She's making it clear that she doesn't intend to stay in the pen with those other pigs, even if they are her littermates.

"Cody, we can't let Rusti keep gettin' out of the pen," Dad says as we all sit on the back porch eating Mom's blackberry cobbler. "Soon, other pigs'll start findin' holes in the fence. It'll be a lot harder to find 'em if they do. They won't know they're supposed to stay near the house. I guess Rusti can live in the yard 'til she gets a little older."

"Yesss!" I exclaim, pumping my fist.

"Dad, you can't be serious," Penny says. "Are you really gonna let that little pig keep livin' in our yard? It'll already be all over school that we have a pig that grunts and wags its tail at the school bus. Besides, who ever heard of namin' a girl pig Rusti?"

"Her name's spelled like a girl's name," I bark at her. "You can just leave her alone."

"That'll be enough from you two," Dad says. "Rusti'll only stay in the yard a little while longer."

Mom whispers to Dad, "And how long is a little while?"

He shrugs his shoulders and shakes his head.

Penny's right about one thing. The next day it is all over school that our pig thinks she's a dog. Knowing Rusti'll be waiting in the yard becomes the highlight of the ride home for the other kids. Some have friends who live in town that ask to ride home with them just so they can see "the funny little pig." They want to see Rusti grunt and wag her tail at the school bus.

Clay tells the other kids, "Our pig's a girl. Her name's Rusti, spelled like a girl's name."

Apparently, Rusti has now become "our pig," even though he never had much to do with her before this.

Some of the older kids on the bus laugh at Rusti and make jokes about her. They call her *hambone* and *pork chop*. One says, "I'll bet she'd be great with eggs for breakfast." Another says, "Yeah, or how 'bout ham steaks on Sunday after church. Yum!"

"C'mon, she's just a little pig," I scold.

"Yeah, looks like a nice, fat, juicy little pig to me," one responds, laughing.

"You guys think you're bein' funny, but I don't think you're funny at all."

"Aw, stop bein' so touchy," another shoots back. "We're just kiddin' around."

It's not kidding to me though, especially about Rusti. It makes me want to pop some of them in the mouth, but that wouldn't solve anything. Besides, they're mostly bigger than me, so the odds are I'd just get beaten up. I wonder if it would have been better if none of the kids on the bus had ever seen her.

Suddenly, a young girl who lives down the

road stands up at the front of the bus and yells, "Y'all need to stop makin' fun of Rusti! She hasn't done anything for you to make fun of her. I think she's cute. Why're you bein' mean to her? Would you like it if everyone laughed at you and made fun of you like that?"

The older kids stop laughing and look embarrassed. Because she has the courage to stand up to them, the older kids seem sorry for the way they're acting. Soon, all the kids are saying nice things about Rusti rather than pointing, laughing, and making fun of her. They shout things like, "Hi, Rusti," "We think you're awesome," and "We love you, Rusti."

Rusti becomes the official mascot for our school bus route. The other kids brag about her to their friends like she's almost as much theirs as she is mine. It's okay though. I like it much better when they're saying nice things about her. And if they all want to claim her as their pet, I think there's probably enough of her to go around.

Chapter Fourteen

The Celebrity

At last the school year ends. WOOHOO!

Rusti rarely stays in her pen now that I'm home most of the time. She eats, sleeps, and hangs out in the yard, spending her days exploring and playing with Bobo and Sancho. She even tries to make friends with Simon. This makes him purr, but he still tries to pretend he doesn't like the attention.

Cars sometimes pull into our driveway. Parents bring their kids to get a look at the pig that acts like a dog. Rusti doesn't disappoint them. She stands in front of the car grunting and wringing her tail. If they get out of the car, Rusti nudges them with her snout. Some of the kids rub her belly and behind her ears. She likes that a lot.

Clay and I laugh. "When did our little pig get to be such a big celebrity?" I ask.

Penny thinks it's humiliating.

By early in the summer, the garden grows more fruits and vegetables than our family can eat. That gives us some produce to sell at our roadside stand. At first, not many people stop to buy what we have to sell. But when parents bring their kids to see Rusti, they also buy fruits and vegetables from the produce stand. Our celebrity, Rusti, is turning into a great "salespig." Fortunately, she isn't demanding a commission—at least not yet. Although, I doubt this celebrity thing will go too much to her head.

Chapter Fifteen

Curiosity

Pigs, in general, are curious animals. They like to inspect almost everything in their path and give special attention to anything that walks or crawls. Rusti takes this natural curiosity to a whole new level. She stops to check out flowers and all kinds of plants, sometimes even giving some of them the taste test. She really likes critters she can watch, follow, and play with.

If she finds a beetle crawling along the ground, Rusti follows it until it disappears underground or into some brush. She likes to find a butterfly and follow its flight. She stands wringing her tail and trying to watch every move the butterfly makes. Pigs don't have very good straight-ahead vision, so she has to concentrate to follow the butterfly with her eyes. She hasn't learned to turn around

when the butterfly flies behind her. Instead, she falls over backward trying to keep watching it. Falling over doesn't faze her at all. She scrambles back up and continues to watch the butterfly until it flies out of sight.

Some of her favorite critters are frogs and toads. When a toad tries to hop away from her, she bounds along after it. When a frog leaps away, she thinks it's playing a game and leaps after it. Pigs are very clumsy jumpers, so she often

stumbles and rolls a few times. This also doesn't bother her a bit. She gets right back up and tries to bounce along after the critter again. Watching her, I laugh until my sides hurt.

One of the most frustrating critters for her is the tortoise. She enjoys finding one because it's so slow and easy to catch. The problem is that the tortoise doesn't want to be caught. Rusti follows it around, but when it draws into its shell, she gets confused. She lies down on her belly near where she has last seen the tortoise's head, grunting and squealing at it.

"What's the matter, Rusti? Doesn't it want to come out and play?" I ask her.

Hearing her name, she looks up at me and then back at the tortoise as if to say, "Where'd it go? Can you make it come back?"

Sooner or later, the tortoise comes out of its shell and tries to escape. Again, Rusti tries to play and touch noses with it. If she gets too close, the tortoise tries to snap at her with its beak. She loses interest in the disagreeable creature after a while, and the tortoise gets away.

The gray squirrel that lives in a big oak tree between the barns and the house is almost as curious as Rusti. When Rusti goes by the tree on her way to or from the barns, the squirrel comes halfway down the trunk, staying high enough to be out of Bobo's reach. It squawks and chatters at Rusti while flicking its bushy tail back and forth. Rusti stops, sits down on her haunches, and grunts at the squirrel. It seems like those two can sit and visit for hours, even though neither has any idea what the other is saying.

We have a peacock that roams around the barns and into the yard. Rusti enjoys following him around. When he fans his tail feathers, Rusti sits on her haunches and stares at his colorful display. The peacock makes a sound that's a lot like a woman's call for help, and Rusti grunts and squeals her response. They can carry on their funny conversation for the longest time.

There are no apparent limits to Rusti's curiosity. Anything and everything is fair game. Her whole world is filled with discovery, amazement, and adventure.

Chapter Sixteen

Coyote

I'm dressed to do my morning chores and about to go out the back door when I hear the most awful noise coming from the yard. Rusti is squealing frantically, and there are strange growling and snarling sounds that I've never heard before.

Dashing out the door, I see Rusti flash by, running for her life. A grayish brown coyote is right on her tail. Rusti scampers and darts around as fast as she can, but her short legs aren't built for speed. The coyote is right behind her, nipping at her and grabbing at her with its front paws. She's scared out of her wits, and as things stand now, it'll only be a matter of time before the coyote catches her. When it does, it'll probably maul her.

"Leave her alone!" I scream as loud as I can. "Get out of our yard."

The coyote pauses for a moment but apparently isn't too impressed with me. I guess a skinny kid isn't much of a threat, especially if the coyote's hungry. It ignores me, returning its attention to Rusti.

I grab the baseball bat on the porch, intending to use it to make the coyote change its breakfast plans. This isn't a well-thought-out plan. Although coyotes generally avoid people, this one could turn and attack me if it thinks I'm trying to steal its prey. But I'm more determined to protect Rusti than I am worried about my own safety.

Suddenly, Bobo comes flying around the side of the house like he was shot out of a cannon. Sancho's several yards behind him, running as fast as his short legs will take him.

"Atta boy, Bobo," I yell. "Sic 'em!"

Bobo slams into the coyote at full speed. The coyote lets out a loud yelp as both animals go tumbling head over heels. They both spring to their feet and square off at each other with hackles raised, fangs bared, and ears pinned back. They

growl at each other, ready for the coming battle.

Sancho catches up, prepared to bravely enter the fight. He circles around behind the coyote, sinks his teeth into one of its back legs, and takes a death grip on the tender hock joint. Again the coyote yelps and spins around. Sancho's action gives Bobo the opening he needs, so he springs onto the coyote's head and bites and clamps onto one of its ears.

The coyote is being attacked from both ends and doesn't know which way to turn. Even Simon has crept up and is crouching in his fiercest attack mode, preparing to jump into the fight whenever he sees an opportunity. It's fortunate for Simon that the opportunity doesn't come.

The coyote manages to free itself from both Bobo and Sancho at the same time. It takes off running as fast as it can, with Bobo in hot pursuit and Sancho trailing. Sancho isn't as fast as the other two, but he makes up for his lack of speed by barking, letting everyone know how loud and ferocious he can be.

I run to Rusti. She's scared and trembling from the attack. She has several scratches on her sides and hind quarter and one sizable cut on her left ham, where it must have caught her with its teeth. But she's better off than she would have been if Bobo and Sancho hadn't come running when they did.

"Don't worry, little girl," I console her. "You're gonna be all right." I run back into the house to get something to doctor her wounds. "Mom, Rusti got attacked by a coyote!" I shout as I come through the back door. "I think she'll be okay, but she has some cuts and scratches I need to take care of." I'm so worried about her that I can't think clearly about what to do next.

"Well, I wondered what all the ruckus was about," Mom says as she gets a basin from under the kitchen sink and fills it with water. To my surprise, Penny, who's already out of bed and dressed, runs into the bathroom and gets rubbing alcohol and antibiotic ointment. She throws a towel over her shoulder, takes the basin of water and soap from Mom, and leads me out the back door.

Dad's already at the barns. With all the noise the other animals make wanting to be fed, he doesn't know about what's going on in the yard.

Clay is still asleep in bed. Mom comes out on the porch to watch Penny and me.

About the time we get to Rusti, the two dogs arrive back in the yard. She comes up and touches noses with Bobo and Sancho as if to say, "Thank you for saving me." Even Simon comes over and gives Rusti a concerned rub before remembering that he doesn't care about anything. He then returns to his perch on the stump, where he can act as if nothing out of the ordinary has happened, licking himself and blinking sleepily.

Penny cleans Rusti's wounds. "Hold her still for me," she tells me as she prepares to apply the alcohol.

It must really sting because Rusti tries to pull away, especially when the alcohol's applied to the cut on her ham. The antibiotic ointment must sooth the sting because she stands still when it's smeared on her wounds.

"None of the scratches are too bad except for the one on her ham," Penny says. "I don't think it'll need stitches, but we'll have to clean it and put ointment on it every day 'til it heals to keep it from getting infected."

"Thanks for takin' care of her," I respond. "You're an awesome sister." I guess she really could be a doctor or something like that someday.

"Bobo, you're such a brave dog," I say as we're finishing up with Rusti. "You sure got after that old coyote. Sancho, you're a fearless beast. You're both very good dogs."

They wag their tails, but both are more focused on what we're doing for Rusti.

When we get through doctoring her, I feed Rusti, Bobo, and Sancho. They all eat hungrily. After breakfast, they celebrate their victory over the coyote by lying down and taking a nap in the yard. Simon and I go on to the barns, so I can do my morning chores just like any other morning, but I don't think I'll ever forget the coyote attack.

Chapter Seventeen

Yowling at the Moon

I'm awakened during the night by a strange sound—a long wailing sound that sort of resembles an ambulance siren. It reminds me of an animal in extreme torment. Lying in bed listening, I can't figure out what kind of animal would be making that awful noise.

The bed in my room is pushed up against a wall with a window. Sometimes during the summer, if it isn't too hot at night, I open the window about halfway and sleep right next to the window sill. I often hear sounds outside my window while I'm drifting off to sleep, but none quite like this.

I slip out of bed, head to the kitchen, and ease out the back door to see what's happening. It's a clear night with a full moon. There, in the middle of the yard, sits Simon. That strange sound is him

yowling up at the moon. It's like he's performing some ancient ritual that's bred into him. I can't keep from laughing at how ridiculous he looks and sounds.

A few minutes later, I see Rusti walk cautiously toward Simon. She nudges him with her snout, as if she's wondering if there's something wrong with him. Who can blame her?

Rusti satisfies herself that he's okay. Well, for Simon, he's as okay as he's going to get. She sits down on her haunches next to him, looks up at the moon, and begins to grunt along with Simon's yowling. Her grunting doesn't quite match the ridiculous sound Simon's making, but it's funny anyway.

Both dogs come from around the side of the house, looking to investigate the weird sounds. Bobo chooses to stay near the porch, a safe distance away, but Sancho saunters over to the other two animals. He sits down next to Rusti. Looking at Simon, he cocks his head comically to one side, looks up at the sky and then back at Simon. He seems to be trying to figure out why stuffy old Simon is acting so strangely.

After watching Simon and Rusti for a while longer, I shake my head. "I'm with you, Sancho," I say. "Simon's a few floats short of a parade. Somebody must've dropped him on his head when he was a kitten. Not sure how he could be much more ridiculous."

I slip through the door and go back to bed. Lying there, I can still hear Simon and Rusti as they continue their hilarious duet. At last, I manage to drift off to sleep.

Chapter Eighteen

Wild Bull Rider

"I have tickets to the rodeo tomorrow night," Dad says as we're eating fresh coconut cake after dinner. "Who wants to go?"

We all raise our hands enthusiastically.

About mid-June each year, a rodeo is held in a town about an hour away. It's a big treat for all of us to go. On the day of the rodeo, I feed all the animals a little earlier than normal. That way, we can leave for the rodeo as soon as Dad gets off work. We try to get there early enough to eat dinner at a restaurant, which we don't normally get to do.

Getting ready is a big part of the fun. Clay and I wear our western shirts with pearl snaps, starched jeans, and freshly polished boots. Penny has a western-style dress that she wears with her boots. Mom and Dad don't go quite as all-out getting dressed up as the rest of us. Mom wears jeans, a nice blouse, and tennis shoes. Dad wears boots and jeans, like he does every day for work, except that his jeans are starched for the rodeo.

We eat at a restaurant that makes delicious hickory-smoked barbecue. Then it's off to the rodeo. We all enjoy the performance, but each of us has our favorite events. Mom and Penny love to watch the girls' barrel racing. The clowns are Clay's favorite. Dad enjoys the team and tie-down roping. My favorite event is bull riding.

Over the years, I've been to many rodeos. But for some reason, this year I feel an extra connection with the bull riders. I'm fascinated by the challenge of a man going up against a bull that's much stronger than him and weighs ten times as much. I also notice the bull riders hang out with some pretty cowgirls. Right then and there, I decide I want to be a professional bull rider.

There's a lot of excited conversation in the car on the way home. They talk about what all they saw and what they liked about the rodeo. Everyone's involved except me, because I'm deep in thought about my newly chosen profession. A couple of times, Mom asks me if I'm feeling okay since I'm being so quiet. I assure her I'm just thinking.

The next day, after I do my morning chores and eat breakfast, I decide to start my new career. I take Rusti, Bobo, Sancho, and Simon to the barns with me for my first training session. First, I have to decide what to do for a bull. There's our Jersey milk cow, but if I try to ride her, she probably won't try to buck me off. She'll just look back at me with her big brown eyes. Besides, who ever heard of a big-time bull rider practicing on a milk cow?

The better option is the Brangus cross steer we're feeding out for beef. He isn't a bull anymore, but he's male. He probably weighs about seven hundred pounds, which is less than half the size of the bulls in the rodeo. I figure that every great bull rider has to start somewhere, so the steer it is for me.

When I watched the bull riders at the rodeo, I noticed they have a rigging that goes around the bull's chest with something to hold onto while they ride. Since I don't have a rigging, I'll have to settle for a rope around the steer's neck.

The dogs, Rusti, Simon, and I go to the steer's pen. It's a five-rail, wood-fenced corral with a shed at one end so the steer can get out of bad weather. Rusti and the dogs wait and watch outside the corral gate, while Simon finds a perch on top of the shed and immediately appears to be dropping off to sleep.

It's easy for me to slip the rope around the steer's neck. He doesn't yet suspect that he's about to become this bull rider's first conquest. I lead him over to the corral fence, step up on the second rail, and hop on his back. He just stands there looking back at me as if to say, "What exactly are you doing?"

I make the fateful decision to "spur" the steer by digging my heels into his sides. Immediately, he bolts. I don't even make it through one jump before I go flying through the air and hit the ground with a thud.

"Oh man, that kind of hurt," I say to Rusti and the dogs. By the way they're looking at me, they think that I've completely lost my mind.

Determined, I pull the steer back to the fence and climb on again. The steer doesn't wait for me to spur him this time. He just takes off. This time, I last about three jumps before being launched in the air and landing with a crack on the bottom rail of the corral fence.

"Ouch. That hurt worse than the first time," I tell my audience. Now all three are standing as they watch the craziness taking place in the corral. "It's all good. I'm sure no great bull rider was successful his first time out," I reason. "It'll just take me a little more practice."

When I try to pull the steer back into position for the next ride, he obviously wants no part of the "fun" we're having. He resists my dragging him near the fence, but with extra pulling on the rope and pushing on his side, I manage to shove him near enough to the fence to step up on the rail and hop on. The steer takes off in a dead run, but this time I actually hang on and stay on his back.

That is, until the steer decides to take this ride to the shed. There's plenty of clearance for the steer to fit under the front side of the shed by himself, but not nearly enough for him to fit under there with me on his back. The two-inch-by-six-inch board at the entrance of the shed hits me right in the chest and skims me off the steer. Simon, who has been perched on the shed, squalls and leaps in the air, hisses at me, and scurries down to the ground. This time, I land with a *splat*, right in a pile of fresh cow manure.

"Oh, *grrross*," I wheeze, trying to catch the breath that's been knocked out of me. By the time I skid to a stop, nasty-smelling cow poop is smeared all the way from the seat of my jeans, up the back of my shirt, and up my neck to the hair on the back of my head. Talk about adding insult to injury.

As I'm lying there in pain, the steer seems to smirk at me as if to say, "And you can stay down there!"

My bull-riding career has ended almost as quickly as it began. It seemed easier and a whole lot more fun when the cowboys at the rodeo did it.

I drag myself across the corral and out the gate, not even feeling like getting to my feet. I sit

for a while against the corral fence with Rusti's head on one leg, Bobo's head on the other leg, and Sancho in my lap. At least they still love me, cow poop and all.

Finally, I manage to get to my feet and limp toward the house. I don't remember it being so far from the barns before. I have to try to sneak in without anyone seeing me and get in the shower before Mom gets home. Then I'll have to bring my clothes back outside and rinse the cow poop off with the garden hose.

"Cody, why're you creepin' around like that?" Dad asks while we're feeding the animals that evening. "You're movin' like you're ninety years old."

"The steer ran over me when I fed him this mornin'." I don't dare tell him what I did. He won't be very happy with me running pounds off the steer, especially doing something as silly as trying my hand at bull riding.

"Need to go to the doctor?" he says, biting his lip and appearing to stifle a laugh.

"No, sir. I just need to be more careful around that steer."

By his reaction, I wonder if Dad knows what really happened. The fact that I forgot to take the rope off the steer's neck might have tipped him off. My dad's seen a lot, and I've learned that it's not easy to pull the wool over his eyes about anything.

Chapter Nineteen

Heaven Scent?

"Bobo, where's your friend?" I say as I go out the back door and into the yard. "Bet she's found some interesting critter to follow around and play with."

I've finished with my morning chores and breakfast, so I have several hours before it's time to tend to my midday chores. During the summer, I make sure all the animals have plenty to drink and spray water under their sheds to help keep them cool through the hot afternoon.

In the yard, I try to think of something fun to do with my extra time. Bobo, Sancho, and Simon are here, but no Rusti. Odd. She tends to stay near the other animals in the yard. I look all around but still don't see her. Then, looking toward the barns, I spot her about halfway between the house and the barns. Sure enough, she's found something to play with, but I can't tell what it is.

As I get closer, I get a better look at her new playmate. *Oh, no.* "No, Rusti! Stop! Don't do that!" I yell, waiving my arms. "You don't wanna play with that! I don't want you to play with that!"

That is a black-and-white-striped skunk!

Rusti looks in my direction but then goes back to playing with the skunk. The skunk isn't making any effort to get away, so Rusti must not pose much of a threat to it. In fact, a couple of times, the two animals go up and sniff noses. It's kind of cute, although *cute* is a relative term when talking about a skunk. *Good*, I think to myself. *If the skunk isn't scared of Rusti, maybe she won't get sprayed.*

Suddenly, Bobo sees the skunk. He lets out a series of barks, raises his hackles, and charges in their direction. Sancho's too short to see what Bobo's seen, but he isn't about to be left out of anything, so off he goes in hot pursuit.

"Bobo! No! Come back!" I scream.

Bobo doesn't hear me or ignores me. Either way, he's on a mission and isn't about to stop.

When the skunk sees Bobo coming, it takes off running toward the trees. Rusti scampers after the skunk, probably thinking they're playing a game. She and Bobo catch up with it at about the same time. The skunk turns and squares off with them as if to say, "You'd better back off if you know what's good for you." Bobo and Rusti seem content to just check the skunk out, so I hope a smelly disaster may still be averted.

Just then Sancho shows up and almost runs the skunk over. Three against one must be too much for the skunk, so it turns away from the dogs and Rusti, throws up its tail, and lets them have it. A yellowish mist sprays out over Bobo, Sancho, and Rusti. While the spray is actually kind of pretty as it glistens in the morning sun, its effects are anything but pretty. The dogs and Rusti turn tail and run back to the yard as fast as they can.

"Peeeeee-yew!" I exclaim as the three of them approach. "You smell awful. You sure messed up this time. Mom and Dad won't be very happy havin' you three stinkers anywhere around. Guess I better see if I can wash some of that smell off."

All three animals are used to being sprayed down with the water hose, but they're not so used to being washed with soap. Doesn't matter. I've got to try to make them smell better, or Mom may not even let them in the yard. I can almost taste that awful skunk smell. Several times it almost makes me gag.

"Oh man," I tell them as I finish with their

baths. "That's 'bout the best I can do to clean you guys up. Y'all still stink, but maybe Mom and Dad won't notice too much."

They notice all right.

"Yuck! Who got into a skunk?" Dad asks as soon as he gets out of his truck. Guess the baths didn't help as much as I hoped.

"Rusti," I reply. "You know how she's always curious about everything, always wantin' to check out other animals? This time, her curiosity got the best of her. Bobo and Sancho got sprayed, too."

"What happened to you?" he asks as he tries to avoid getting too close to any of us. "You don't smell so good yourself."

"I gave 'em all baths to try to wash off some of the smell."

"Your mom will be so proud of all four of you," says Dad. "I hope Rusti's curiosity doesn't ever cause her to find somethin' that can really hurt her, like a rattlesnake or somethin' like that."

As I go into the house for supper, Mom catches me before I get a few feet in the door. "Cody, what's that awful smell? You get sprayed by a skunk?"

"No, ma'am. Rusti and the dogs did."

"Well, what did you do, get down and wallow with 'em?" she asks.

Dad laughs, which earns him pursed lips and a stern glare from Mom.

"No, ma'am. I gave 'em all baths. Guess I got some of the skunk smell on me."

"Guess you did, too," she shoots back. "Get out of those smelly clothes and get in the shower right now. Wash several times with soap, and shampoo your hair at least three times. We can't even stand to have you at the dinner table smelling like that. I'll probably have to burn your clothes. Heavens, what am I going to do with the whole bunch of you?"

I take my third shower later that evening. I hope Rusti's curiosity will be satisfied with less stinky things, like butterflies and frogs, from now on. When she plays with those other critters, I don't have to take so many showers. I'll probably end up taking as many showers today as I'd normally take in a whole week.

Chapter Twenty

Ferocious Rodent

What in the world is that cat playing with? I wonder as I pull weeds in the garden. Simon, who's always very reserved, is as animated as I've ever seen him. He's in the yard near the garden, lying on his belly with something trapped between his front paws. His tail flicks back and forth, his neck is arched, and all his attention is focused on whatever he's found.

When he gently nudges it with his nose, I get a look at it. A small, brown field mouse. Simon isn't trying to eat it. Instead, he catches it, releases it so it scampers several inches away, and then pounces on it—over and over again. To him, the rodent is just a fun toy. From what I can see, except for some cat saliva on its fur, the mouse isn't much worse for the wear. Simon seems very proud of himself for being such a great hunter, and I can't help but laugh out loud as he pounces on the poor creature again.

Rusti and the dogs are now very interested in what Simon's doing. Rusti is lying on her belly watching to see what Simon will do next, probably hoping the mouse will be something for her to follow and play with. Bobo and Sancho stand nearby, intent on Simon's discovery and waiting for their own chance with the mouse.

A few feet away, Penny's lying on a lounge chair in her swim suit "getting some sun." If you ask me, she'd get plenty of sun if she spent more time outside instead of watching TV and sending text messages to her friends. When I start laughing, she looks over at us. "What's your silly cat doin' now?"

Simon releases the mouse again and it tries to scamper away.

"Oh my gosh!" she shrieks. "He's got a mouse!"

Simon startles at her shout and jumps backward. His retreat gives the little mouse an unexpected opening to escape, and it dashes right toward Penny. She jumps up from the lounge

chair and gives a deafening scream that scares Rusti and both dogs. They dart off in the opposite direction with their heads down and tails between their legs. Rusti runs so fast that she stumbles and rolls before bouncing up to continue her escape.

Penny takes off, trying to get away from the ferocious little field mouse. No matter which way she goes, the frightened mouse scampers right toward her—and it's *gaining* on her! With the way she's screeching and going on, you'd think it was a giant rat or some monster you'd see at the movies. It's a tiny field mouse for crying out loud.

I'm laughing so hard that I can barely catch my breath. I can't even stay standing and end up lying in the grass, howling. Bobo, Sancho, and Rusti have arrived at what they hope is a safe distance away. Peeking around some bushes, they're doing their best to stay clear of the fearsome beast that's terrorizing the entire yard. Simon has disappeared, having obviously decided he's had enough fun with his mouse toy.

At last, the mouse takes off in the opposite direction from my screaming sister. It may have gone into the garden, but it's difficult for me to see through eyes that are blurred with tears from laughing so hard.

Penny figures out that the mouse is no longer chasing her. When I finally stop laughing so hard and get up from the grass, I see her storming through the back door into the house. Bobo, Sancho, and Rusti slowly creep out from their hiding place, hoping the terrifying danger has passed. Simon still hasn't decided it's safe—we might not see him again until supper.

If Penny gets that excited about a field mouse, how might the drama queen act if something really scary comes after her? Hmmm, that makes me think. I wonder what other critter I might find to recreate this amusing spectacle—except next time, it needs to be something that will stick around a while and won't run into the garden at the first opportunity. If I can work it out right, such an event could be better than watching TV or even going to a movie.

Chapter Twenty-one

Growing Up

Bobo and Sancho were full grown when Rusti was born. Rusti, on the other hand, is a growing young female pig. By midway through the summer, she is already almost the height of Bobo and close to fifteen pounds heavier. Her growth rate is right where it should be for a healthy developing pig.

Even so, her growth has changed the way she and the dogs play games in the yard. Instead of Rusti and Sancho chasing Bobo, more often Rusti is now being chased by the two dogs. She isn't as fast or nimble as Bobo, but she has become quicker on her feet.

Sometimes Clay joins in their game. He runs, laughing his head off, with the three animals chasing him all around the yard. At some

point during the chase, Sancho manages to trip him, and all four of them end up in a pile out in the grass. Rusti sometimes tries to get Simon involved, but the game is too foolish for him.

Mom, Dad, and even Penny enjoy watching these hilarious games of tag. Dad lets out one of his big belly laughs and says, "That has to be the craziest thing I ever saw. Two dogs, a pig, and a kid runnin' around and playin' like wild banshees!"

During their games, I get the water hose out and spray Rusti, Bobo, and Sancho. People are able to sweat to help keep them from becoming overheated. Dogs and pigs don't sweat, so spraying the animals with the water hose prevents them from getting too hot in the summer sun. Besides, it's a lot of fun to watch them splash around in the water and slide through the mud they make.

Chapter Twenty-two

Fowl Play

"Better settle down if you know what's good for you," I warn our Rhode Island Red rooster as I walk toward the hen house to gather eggs. "Don't start none, won't be none!"

The barnyard bully is staring me down in his most intimidating attack posture: head down, neck feathers flared out, and wings low. One of his favorite activities is attacking anyone or anything that dares to venture into the hen house and surrounding area.

His normal approach is to fly at the intruder, slap with his wings, try to cut with his spurs, and peck with his beak. His spurs aren't as damaging now since Dad filed them down, but he still uses them to jab at his victims. He can cause some ugly bruises with his powerful wings, and he's capable of drawing blood wherever he pecks with his beak.

The rooster and I have a kind of truce. He likes to pretend he might try to attack me, but we both know it's all for show. As long as he doesn't come after me, I won't have to use my feet to defend myself. He knows I've got his number, and I'm not afraid to dial it up if I need to.

The other animals have no such understanding with this *fowl* creature. The dogs and Simon avoid going near the hen house. On the occasions when they do get too close to his domain, the fight is on! It's hilarious to see big, tough Bobo tuck tail and run with the red rooster in hot pursuit. You'd think a ferocious dog-mauler was after him, instead of a seven-pound, winged marauder.

Poor Sancho yelps to high heaven and runs for his life. Simon tries to play tough and face down the rooster by arching his back, hissing, and batting at it with his front claws, but his stand against the rooster's attack doesn't last long. Soon he jumps up on the roof of one of the outbuildings or runs up a tree to safety. The rooster rules the roost around the barnyard, and he knows it.

Too bad nobody has told Rusti about the danger that lurks near the hen house. When she ventures with me to the barns, most of the time she stays with the dogs. But today, she decides to follow me to the hen house. By the way the rooster's puffed up in his attack posture, Rusti hasn't escaped his attention.

"Rusti, you'd better watch that ol' rooster," I tell her. "He'll be all over you like scales on a fish."

She treats the rooster like this will be a new adventure with yet another fascinating playmate. She saunters up to the battle-braced bird and stretches out her neck to try to touch noses with him. Her innocent advance earns her a sharp peck on the snout. She startles and backs away a little, but after a few moments, she moves closer and dances around the rooster, leaping and twisting.

This show of friendly playfulness doesn't impress the rooster. With his neck feathers flared out, he flies at Rusti's head, beating her with his wings, striking at her with his spurs, and pecking her on the snout.

The attack startles Rusti again. She sits back on her haunches with a look of bewilderment on her

cute face, her long eyelashes flutter in disbelief.

The rooster attacks her head again. This time Rusti responds by good-naturedly batting him away with her snout. The rooster awkwardly flutters and flops several feet away. He leaps to his feet and shakes dust from his feathers, clearly surprised that an intruder has fended off his attack.

Again, Rusti approaches the rooster and he flies at her head. She easily swats him away. The rooster lets out sharp clucking sounds and tries to appear as scary as possible as he circles Rusti. This isn't how things are supposed to work when an outsider comes into his turf. On the other hand, Rusti appears to think they're playing a game, even if it is a little different from the games she plays with the other animals.

Rusti dances around the rooster. He makes his most ferocious attack yet, but the result doesn't change. She swats him away with added gusto. He lands even farther away, tumbling and flopping and stirring up a cloud of dust. This time, the rooster doesn't bother to shake the dust from his feathers. He picks himself up and makes a mad dash into the hen house. She follows him and stands at the hen house door, peering in to see where her new playmate's gone. As far as she's concerned, the game just started to be fun, and she's ready to play some more.

"Rusti, I think that ornery ol' rooster's met his match with you," I say, laughing, as I finish gathering the eggs. "Funny thing is you didn't even know you were in a fight. Think I'll bring you with me every time I gather eggs from now on. You can be my personal bodyguard."

I don't think that feisty rooster will soon forget the thrashing he took from the snout of a young red pig. Maybe he'll learn that he shouldn't go around picking fights. You don't make many friends that way, and, sooner or later, you might run into someone that'll flat-out clean your plow.

Chapter Twenty-three

Garden Visitor

"Cody, I want you to pick a mess of green beans for supper," Mom says as we're finishing breakfast one morning.

Working in the garden is a daily chore for me during the summer months. There's always something to do. My favorite days are watering days, which are about every other day. The days we water are kind of like a day off because the soil gets too muddy for me to do anything else. On the other days, I pick produce and chop weeds. After I pick the beans today, I'll give them to Penny. She'll wash and snap them, and they'll be ready to cook for supper this evening.

I'm not exactly sure how many beans equal a "mess." When we sell beans at the produce stand, we sell them by the pound or sometimes by the half bushel. We don't sell an amount we call a *mess*. How much is in a mess varies a lot, depending on whether it's beans, peas, squash, corn, or whatever vegetable we might be picking. Best I can figure, a mess is about how much we'll eat at one meal.

Fresh green beans are one of my favorite things to eat, but I'm not too wild about picking them. Unlike some vegetables, green beans don't grow on the top of the plant. I have to squat down by the bean vines, raise them up, and pick the beans from the underside of the plant. The work is slow and boring.

When I go to the garden to gather the beans, I carry my picking basket and a hoe I've sharpened to cut any weeds I find. In thirteen years, I've picked a lot of beans. It doesn't really take a lot of concentration, and sometimes I daydream about all kinds of things. I especially like to think about my friend Hannah, the pretty girl I see at the livestock shows.

While lost in one of my daydreams, I hear a sound that brings me laser-focused back to what I'm doing. I fall backward, plopping down on my butt. I use the heels of my boots to quickly scoot several feet away from the sound. My heart's pounding, my mouth goes dry, and I can feel the hair on the back of my neck standing up.

The sound is kind of like a baby's rattle being slightly shaken. But having heard the sound before, I know it isn't a baby's rattle. It's a rattlesnake. It's warning me that it knows I'm here and that I should stay away. It was probably slithering through the cool shade of the garden plants, looking for an easy meal, like a mouse feeding on the vegetables.

After scrambling to my feet, I search for the rattler from a distance. Its coloring blends in well with the ground and plants, and I can't find it. Leaving my picking basket on the ground, I go back to the end of the row to get my hoe. I also make sure the dogs and Rusti are on the outside of the fence and the gate's securely closed. The last thing I need right now is to have to keep curious Rusti away from this snake.

When I get back to where I was picking, I poke around the bean plants with the business-end of the hoe to see if I can get the snake to rattle. Nothing. The only thing worse than finding a

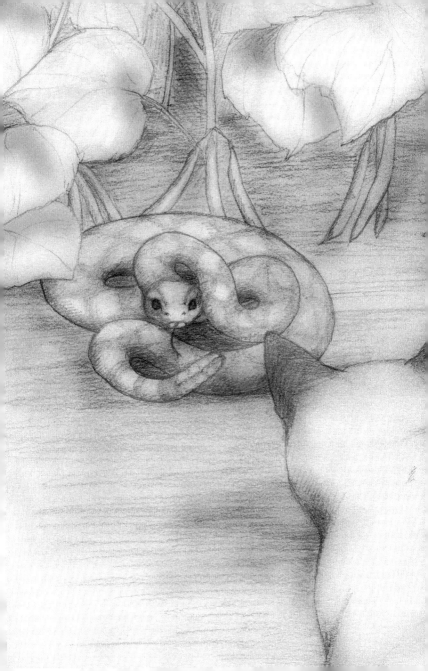

rattler in the garden is knowing there's one there but not being able to find it.

A couple of rows away, I notice Simon crouched in attack mode with his tail twitching back and forth. Not surprisingly, Simon has found the diamondback rattlesnake. It's about three and a half feet long, which isn't huge, but it's plenty big enough to be deadly. The rattler is coiled, watching Simon with beady dark eyes and flicking its tongue up and down, sizing him up. Simon inches closer, and the snake's rattle begins to buzz a warning. In no time, Simon's less than a foot from its head, which is cocked and ready to strike.

Suddenly, the rattler strikes with its wide-open, white mouth and deadly fangs. Simon squalls and leaps about three feet straight up in the air. When he lands, he comes down right on top of the now-angry snake. Without recoiling, the rattler strikes at Simon again. The cat jumps again, this time landing several feet away and out of striking distance—lucky for him.

"There's a thin line between bravery and stupidity, and you went way passed it this time," I tell Simon. Now I have to figure out what to do about the rattlesnake that's in a very foul mood after Simon's attack.

Rattlesnakes usually aren't aggressive. They would rather leave people alone and be left alone. When I happen upon one out in open pasture land where people don't usually go, I leave it be. If this snake wanted to be left alone it should have stayed away from the garden, out in the open pasture. Now leaving it alone is not an option.

Bobo, Sancho and Rusti sense that there's something unusual going on. They stand intently watching at the fence.

I break off a corn stalk that's finished producing and use it to try to ease the snake's head away from its coiled body, all the while staying out of striking distance. This isn't easy to do. The rattler is a tightly coiled ball of muscle that isn't the least bit interested in being pulled around. A couple of times it strikes at the corn stalk, but I'm sure its tongue tells it the corn stalk isn't the target it's looking for. Finally, I get the snake's head pulled far enough away from its body to take a one-handed swing at it with the hoe. The snake moves just as the hoe is coming down, so I only get a partial cut on its body behind its head.

Now the rattler's injured and really mad. The snake's rattles are whirring and vibrating so fast they become a blur. Bobo and Sancho are barking, Rusti is pacing up and down the fence squealing and grunting, and Simon starts moving back into position to renew his attack. I can smell the pungent, musky odor of the rattler.

It strikes at anything that moves. The snake's white mouth flashes in my direction with fangs that look like they might be an inch long. No longer trying to maneuver the snake's head, I chop furiously at any part of the snake I can hit. On the third chop, I hit right behind the snake's head and sever it from the rest of its body.

I've heard that a rattler's head can still strike for about an hour after it has been cut off, so I dig a hole with the hoe and bury the head. Then I cut off the rattles with my pocket knife, so I'll have a souvenir. This will make a great story later.

My heart rate is slowing back to normal, and I can finally make enough saliva to swallow. With the excitement subsiding, I remember I still have a mess of green beans to pick. I cautiously resume my picking and give the beans to Penny when I've finished.

Going back into the yard near the garden, I tie a string on what's left of the rattler's body and tease Simon with it. Backing away from the snake body with the string in my hand, I twitch the snake slightly to get Simon's attention. When he approaches the snake in attack mode, I wait until he gets right up to it and then give the string a big jerk. Simon leaps high in the air, like when the snake struck at him. I have fun teasing him for a while. Afterward, I bury the rattler's body.

That evening as we have chocolate pie after supper, I tell my family about my ruckus with the rattler and show off the rattles. Dad likes the part about what he calls "Simon's misguided bravado" and thinks the whole story's pretty funny. That is, until he sees the stern look on Mom's face.

"What was a rattlesnake doing in our garden?" she demands.

"Well, I don't know," answers Dad. "I sure didn't put it there." He glances at me. "We sometimes find a bull snake or hognose snake out there, don't we?"

I nod in agreement.

"We don't bother 'em 'cause they eat mice and other varmints feedin' on our vegetables," Dad continues. "We hardly ever see a rattlesnake in the garden. They usually stay in the pasture. But if one decides to come into the garden, there's not a whole lot I can do to stop it." He turns to us kids. "You'll need to be careful and watch for snakes from now on."

"I don't think I even want to go in the garden anymore," Penny says.

"You'll go," Dad counters. "That can't be an excuse for not doin' your share of the chores."

"Just what I need, something else to worry about," Mom says, looking even more worried. "The last thing I want is one of you gettin' snake bit."

It probably would've been a better idea if I'd told only Dad about the rattlesnake and let him decide when and how to break the news to Mom. Besides helping me become a rattlesnake wrangler, this experience has taught me a lesson in timing.

Chapter Twenty-four

Town Kid

"Cody, I have a co-worker who has a son about your age," Mom says, speaking some of the most dreaded words of the summer. "I told her she can bring him out here to work with you for a day. I want you to let him have a taste of what it's like to live on a farm."

I know from past experiences that it won't do me any good to argue with her.

We're finishing up breakfast on what started out looking like a perfect summer day, but now it's probably ruined. About two or three times every summer, Mom gets to talking with a co-worker, somebody from church, or even someone she meets at the grocery store, and she tells them to bring their kids out to our place to learn about farming.

Every now and then, the kid who shows up is fun to hang out with for a day, but most times that's not the case. Usually, it's a kid who's used to sitting around the house all day complaining about being bored, and I end up becoming a babysitter for the day.

Not long after Mom leaves for work, the kid's mom drops him off. I recognize him from school. His name is Tommy. He's a year younger than me and not someone I would choose to hang out with. At school, he's usually doing something goofy and acting kind of immature for his age. But like it or not, I'm stuck with him today.

This morning, Dad and I moved some sows from one pen to another so they'll be able to graze in a new pasture. Doing that threw off my schedule for morning chores, so I asked Dad if I could wait until after breakfast to milk the cow. The first thing I have to do now is get the milking done. Tommy follows me to the barns.

I get the cow in the milking shed and start milking her. When I look up, Tommy's at the back of the cow, pumping her tail up and down like you might see in a cartoon. He's laughing his head off. This kind of thing might have been funny to me when I was five or six—or maybe not even then. Now it's just annoying for me and the cow. She looks at him with her big brown eyes as if to say, "What exactly do you think you're doing?" It makes me wish I had some way to signal to the cow that this would be a good time for her to poop or pee all over him.

After I finish the milking, I give Simon his dish of milk and take the rest to Penny so she can take care of it.

"What are we gonna do now?" Tommy asks.

"I need to pick some corn and tomatoes for the roadside stand," I tell him. I doubt that he'll be any more help with this chore than he was with the milking, but I get two baskets for the produce as we head out for the garden.

I pick the corn while he just stands there watching me. I show him how to tell when an ear of corn is ready to be picked. First, you look at the ear to see if it's begun to lean away from the stalk. Then, you feel the ear to see if it's full all the way to the tip and look at the silks coming out the end of the ear to see if they're brown and dry.

Next, I pick tomatoes. There's not much of a secret to picking tomatoes. When they're mostly red, they're ready to be picked. I've just started picking the tomatoes when I look up in time to see Tommy throw a ripe tomato at Rusti and the dogs. It hits Sancho right on the head and Tommy laughs hysterically. Sancho runs to the fence with his tail between his legs and looks at me as if to say, "What did I do?"

That does it. Tommy's wasting perfectly good food, and he's mistreating my animals. He needs to learn a lesson he wasn't counting on. "Have you ever sucked eggs?" I ask him.

He gives me a skeptical look and shakes his head.

"It's a really cool thing to do," I say. "But you've got to be a special kind of person to do it. I'm not sure you're that kind of person. No, probably not. Never mind."

"Betcha I am," Tommy responds. "I wanna try it. *Please.*"

"Well, I guess it'll be okay. C'mon." I leave my baskets in the garden and lead Tommy back to the hen house.

When we get to the hen house, I go in to see if any more eggs have been laid since I gathered them earlier this morning. I find two that have probably been laid in the last thirty minutes or so. Taking out my pocket knife, I peck a small hole in the shell in the small end of one of the eggs. I put the index finger of my left hand over the hole and turn the egg over, then peck a larger hole in the big end of the egg.

"The small hole will allow air in the eggshell," I explain. "You put your mouth over the large hole, tilt your head back, take your finger off the small hole, and suck the egg into your mouth." I show him how it's done.

There's something important to know when you suck an egg. You have to suck the egg out of the shell and swallow it all in one motion. If you get the egg stuck in your mouth, it becomes almost impossible to swallow. Eventually, you'll break the yolk in your mouth and then it just seems to get bigger and bigger. Having experience with this kind of thing, I managed to suck my egg with no problem.

I hand my knife over to Tommy, along with

his egg. He pecks the hole in the small end of the egg and puts his finger over the hole, just like I showed him. Then he turns the egg over and pecks a larger hole in the big end, following my directions exactly. He puts his mouth over the large hole, tilts his head back, and sucks the egg into his mouth. But he doesn't swallow. His cheeks are all puffed out, and I soon see the golden egg yolk trickling out of the corners of his mouth and heading toward his chin.

I've got him! He doesn't know what to do. Then I see tears running down his cheeks. *Aw, man.* I wasn't expecting it would make him cry.

He spits out the egg and runs back to the house without saying a word to me. I watch as he enters the back door, then I decide to finish picking the tomatoes. While I'm in the garden, I start feeling guilty for being mean to Tommy. He probably deserved it for the way he was treating the animals, but that doesn't make it right. Besides, what if he got sick from the egg? On my way from the garden to the produce stand, I stop by the house to make sure he's okay. He's sitting on the couch watching TV with Clay, looking perfectly content. That's probably where he should have been anyway.

I take the corn and tomatoes to the roadside stand. We have a sign up that tells people to honk their horn, and somebody will come out to sell them produce. But sometimes, I like to sit out here with Rusti, Bobo, Sancho, and Simon, especially when I have free time and don't want to be in the house. This is one of those times.

Sometime in the middle of the afternoon, a car pulls into the driveway and picks up Tommy. He seems happy to have been here and waves good-bye to all of us.

At dinner that evening, Mom seems distant. She probably hasn't said more than two words through the whole meal. This might not be a good sign. She hands me a big hunk of chocolate cake with chocolate icing—one of my all-time favorite desserts—then breaks her silence. "Cody, I got a call from the mother of the boy who spent the day here today."

Uh-oh. I drop my fork before I get to take the first bite of cake.

"Did you make that poor boy suck an egg?"

Aw, man. He went home and tattled on me. Dad starts chuckling but is trying not to laugh, and Penny and Clay are giggling.

"Well, I didn't make him do it," I respond. "He said he wanted to. Besides, you told me to give him a taste of farming."

Dad busts out with a big belly laugh. He's not helping my situation at all.

Mom's not laughing or even smiling. "You know that's not what I meant." She then glares at Dad for laughing.

"Yes, ma'am." I know there's no use trying to defend myself or telling her what Tommy was doing.

"His mom told me he was really enjoying himself and learning a lot from you before the egg incident," Mom continues.

Humph, sure could've fooled me, I think.

"Cody, here on the farm you get to do and see things every day that other kids can't even imagine. You like farming, and you have a great way of explaining what you do to other people when you want to. Don't you think you can be nicer and more understanding with kids who are trying to learn something from you? Isn't that the way you want to be treated when you're trying to learn something new?"

"Yes, ma'am," I reply. "I'll try to be more patient next time." But I sure hope the next time isn't anytime soon.

There's no more discussion about Tommy, but the whole thing has soured my appetite, even for chocolate cake.

Chapter Twenty-five

Stock Pond Swimming

"Hey, guys. Wanna go swimmin'?" I ask the dogs, Rusti, and Simon one afternoon after I've finished my midday chores.

Bobo and Sancho jump around, acting like they know what swimming is, but they're probably happy to go anywhere and do just about anything. So Bobo, Sancho, Simon, Rusti, and I set out to beat the heat of the day in a neighbor's stock pond.

The pond is kept full by a windmill that pumps water from an underground well. It gives the neighbor's cattle a place to get a drink and cool off from the heat. Cows almost always come to drink in the early morning and late in the evening, so they're rarely here when we come to swim. The pond isn't very deep, about ten feet at the deepest place and shallow around the edges.

The first thing I do is cannonball into the water and dive to the bottom where it's coolest. When I come up for air, I call the other four in to join me. Rusti comes into the water but stays in the shallow part that only comes halfway up her side. Bobo jumps right in. Sancho's a little more reluctant. But, not wanting to be left out, he bounds in after Bobo. Simon wouldn't even think about doing something foolish like going swimming. Besides, he'd get wet, and that isn't about to happen. He sits on the bank and watches us, licking his paws and pretending to have no interest in what we're doing.

The two dogs follow me everywhere I swim, dog-paddling along, even across the deepest part of the pond. After cooling off some, I swim into the shallow water and splash Rusti. Bobo and Sancho pick up on this game. They run, leap into the water, and splash everyone, including Simon, which makes him climb up on the windmill for a safer spot to watch. Rusti dives down into the water and then comes up and slings water and mud on everyone. Swimming with my friends is

an awesome way to cool off and spend a hot summer afternoon.

At supper I get busted by Mom. "You've been swimmin' in that nasty old stock pond again, haven't you? You reek of pond water. I guess you know the cows probably poop and pee in that water."

Ugh. Don't guess I've ever thought about that. Makes me wonder if I ever had my mouth open while I was underwater. Oh well. Rusti and the dogs don't seem to mind, so I guess it doesn't bother me either.

"As soon as you finish supper, get yourself in the shower," Mom says. "Be sure to wash your hair and clean down in your ears. Cody, I love you, but sometimes I think I must be raisin' some kind of savage."

I'm not sure what it means to be "some kind of savage," but if it includes swimming in a stock pond, it must be a pretty good way to live. The dogs, Rusti, and I like it anyway.

Chapter Twenty-six

Sheep Thrills

"What's that noise?" I take a quick glance over my shoulder as I walk from the barns to the house after finishing my chores on a beautiful summer morning.

There's my answer. Following a little ways behind me is a young Southdown lamb. "Uh-oh. Got a sheep out."

Every year, my family buys enough lambs so Penny, Clay, and I have two each for our 4-H lamb projects. We try to get a variety of breeds, but we always have a good Southdown lamb. A friend of ours raises that breed, so he saves us a lamb he thinks may be a champion in the show ring.

Young lambs are pretty high on the cuteness scale, and Southdown lambs are even cuter than most. Their fleece, face, and legs are all white.

Their most adorable feature is that they're smaller than most other breeds of sheep. When they're young, Southdown lambs look like huggable stuffed animals.

It looks like I'll have to go back to the barns to see how the lamb got out of the sheep pen. I'll then need to pen it back up and fix the fence so it can't get out again. But I'm starving for breakfast after my morning chores, and it may take a while for me to get the repairs done. If I take care of the lamb right now, I might not get to eat breakfast until almost lunchtime.

While I'm trying to figure out what to do, the dogs, Rusti, and Simon come to check out the escaped lamb. The dogs approach and sniff it, but they've seen lots of lambs, so their interest is brief. Simon is also curious about the lamb. He gets as close as he can without appearing to be too curious.

On the other hand, Rusti is completely curious. She greets the lamb as if it might bring her a fantastic new adventure, grunting at it and stretching forward to touch noses with it. At first, the lamb doesn't know what to think of Rusti and doesn't share her friendliness. It tries to get away from her, but she isn't the least bit put off and follows right behind it.

Rusti clearly isn't a threat, and the lamb eventually responds by leaping playfully. This is exactly the kind of fun Rusti has in mind, so she joins the jumping around. Soon she and the lamb are engaged in a kind of dance that is nothing short of entertaining. They bound up and down, twist around, and chase each other beneath a big oak tree. After several minutes of play time, they lay on their bellies in the shade, staring admiringly at each other. They rest a while and then start their dance over again. It's amazing watching them play together this way; they've just met. They're like two peas in a pod.

It seems that Rusti might be able to keep the lamb occupied long enough for me to run in the house and grab a bite to eat. After I get some breakfast, I'll go back to the barns and see how he got out.

I choke down a quickly whipped-up breakfast sandwich made with a biscuit, sausage, and jelly, then jog back to the barns. When I get there, I

see where the lamb squeezed between the gate post and gate of the sheep pen. I don't need to fix the fence. I just need to adjust the gate so the gap between the gate post and gate is too small for the lamb to slip through.

After I finish adjusting the gate, I go back to the yard to get the lamb and return it to the sheep pen. Rusti and the lamb are still dancing. I can't resist standing there a while, watching them and laughing. They're now jumping and twisting in a synchronized dance that almost looks like it's been staged.

Dad returns from buying feed in town. "Why's that lamb out of the sheep pen?" he asks as he gets out of his truck. "You gonna catch it and pen it back up or just stand there gawkin' at it?"

"Oh, it figured out how to squeeze between the gate and gate post," I say. "I got the gate adjusted so it won't be able to do it anymore. Could that lamb and Rusti be any cuter together? They've been doin' this little dance of theirs for 'bout an hour."

Dad stands beside me, and we watch and laugh at the two animals for several minutes. Then he says, "Cody, you know we can't have all our animals livin' in the yard, right? We may be testin' your mom's patience with Rusti still livin' up here. The lamb will have to go back to the pen."

"Yes, sir. I'll catch it and take it back right now."

Rusti doesn't understand what I'm doing when I pick up the little lamb to take it back to the pen. She follows me all the way to the sheep pen, grunting and squealing at the little lamb. When I put the lamb back in the pen, Rusti stands at the fence and touches noses with it. She grunts at it and it bleats back at her. They aren't at all ready to give up their fun and friendship so soon.

I wish I could keep the little lamb in the yard to play with Rusti. I can only imagine the adventures they could have together.

Chapter Twenty-seven

Watermelon Games

"Cody, you wanna go get those watermelons so we can cut 'em?" Dad asks one afternoon as we finish dinner. "Be sure you don't *accidentally* drop one and eat the heart out of it before anybody else gets any."

"You don't really think I'd do such a thing," I respond, grinning.

Dad knows it won't be the first time if I do.

We raise sweet watermelons out in our market garden, selling many of them from the roadside stand during the summer. But the watermelons are also a tasty treat for our family. About every other morning, I pick two watermelons out of the garden, choosing ones that are sure to be sweet and juicy. I put them in a pool of cool water that forms near the water well, and by late in the afternoon, they're cooled to a perfect temperature for after-supper dessert.

When I bring the melons to Dad, he splits them lengthwise down the middle. They're large melons with enough sweet heart meat for everyone. We each take a large piece in our fingers. It's very juicy, and soon we all have sticky watermelon juice dripping from our chins and running from our hands to our elbows. We laugh at each other as we try to eat the melon without getting the juice all over us.

After we've eaten our fill, the watermelon games begin. First the seed-spitting contest. It's not as much spitting as it is making your mouth look like you're trying to whistle; you blow the seed out. I've been practicing, and I'm getting some good distance on my seeds. But Dad's the champion seed-spitter in our family. I've learned some very important lessons from this contest, like make sure the wind is behind you instead of blowing toward you. Otherwise, the seed won't go far, and if the wind's strong enough, you may end up wearing the seeds you're spitting.

Next, we have an all-out watermelon war. We grab clods of the remaining watermelon and chase each other with them. They can be thrown at others, but the most fun is squeezing the melon clods so the sticky juice squirts on someone else. Mom and Dad insist that they don't want to be included in this game, so they stand on the porch and watch the craziness.

Penny also says she doesn't want to be part of the watermelon war, but Clay and I don't listen. We love squeezing watermelon juice in her hair, which makes her scream and whine, "Mom, make 'em stop. Now I'll have to wash my hair!"

"Cody, stop pickin' on your sister," Mom scolds.

"It serves you right for sittin' on me and ticklin' me when we were younger," I respond, laughing. "I told you I wouldn't always be littler than you." No one gets too worried about her hair. We all know she washes her hair every night anyway.

Bobo and Sancho like to watch these games from the sidelines with Mom and Dad. It gets too wild even for them, and Simon sits as far away as he can, while still being able to watch the action.

Rusti doesn't mind a little craziness. She jumps

right into the action, hoping to join in the fun. Clay and I oblige by chasing her and squeezing juice on her. Unlike the rest of us, she doesn't mind getting sticky. Next, we throw the watermelon clods at her. She tastes one of the clods that misses her and finds she really likes it. After that, when watermelon clods are thrown at her, she stops, sits on her back haunches, and tries to catch them, which makes us laugh out loud. We decide to launch watermelon clods at Rusti to see if she can catch them in her mouth. They hit her not only in the mouth but also on her nose, in her ears, and pretty much everywhere else. Soon, she is one sticky, watermelon-juice-mess of a pig.

When the watermelon games are over, Dad makes all three of us kids and Rusti stand out in the yard while he squirts us with the garden hose to rinse off the juice. Rusti likes this part of the games a lot. Really, we all do. Even Bobo and Sancho get involved in the hosing-off part of the games because it's hot and it helps them cool off. Simon, who makes sure to keep a safe distance during the games, vanishes when the hose comes out. He isn't about to get wet.

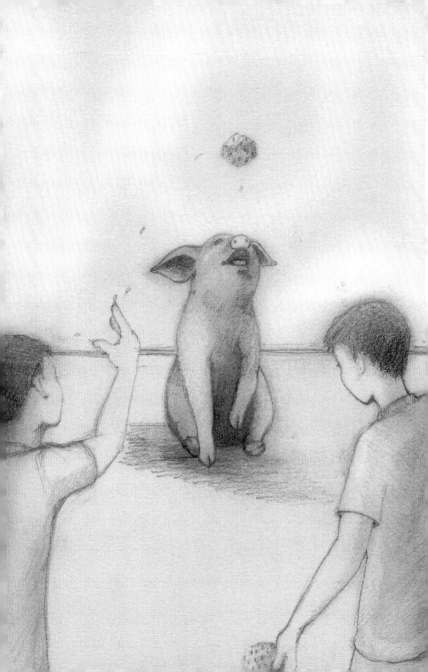

Our family has a great time taking part in the watermelon games—or even just watching them. They're one of the ways we have fun as a family. Besides, we have a blast getting all sticky.

Chapter Twenty-eight

End of Summer

Summer is now winding down, and Bobo, Sancho, Rusti, and Simon follow me to the barns most days when I do my chores. Rusti's about five months old. Instead of eating in the yard, she now eats from a trough along the fence of a pen where pigs her age live. She seems to enjoy standing at the fence and talking to the other pigs. She's learned to communicate with Bobo, Sancho, Simon, and even me, although we speak different languages. But here are pigs that speak her language. She lingers at the barns and visits with the other pigs even when the dogs, Simon, and I start back to the house.

She also likes to go over to the sheep pen. None of the lambs in the pen have any interest in Rusti, except the Southdown lamb. The two

of them stand at the fence touching noses, with Rusti grunting and the lamb bleating. It's amazing that they still remember each other after that one time they played together in the yard.

The time is soon approaching when my family will prepare to take our 4-H pigs and lambs to show at the fall stock shows. Rusti has become a fine-looking gilt. She's long and tall, her muscling is well developed, and she's built solid and sound. At about two hundred pounds, she's almost full grown.

"Are we gonna take Rusti to the stock shows?" I ask Dad one evening. We've done our afternoon chores and now stand together looking over the show animals.

"We definitely want to take her to the shows," Dad responds. "She might be the best animal we have on the place. It's important for the reputation of our farm to take the best we have. We won't sell her. We'll bring her home and breed her to raise show pigs that might be future prizewinners. But we want other farmers to see her and know the kind of quality show animals we raise on this farm. The other farmers might wanna buy some of our other pigs 'cause they hope to get one like her."

"What if another farmer at the stock show tries to buy her?" I ask. "I don't want her to go to a farm she doesn't know. There might be people there who don't know how special she is."

Dad laughs. "It'd be a possibility. There are lots of farmers who'd pay a handsome price for a fine-lookin' animal like Rusti. They could probably raise prize-winning pigs of their own from one like her. But we'll bring her home and keep her right here."

Chapter Twenty-nine

Stock Show

We're preparing to take our 4-H pig and lamb projects to the county livestock show and fair. This isn't the biggest stock show we'll attend this fall, but it's an important one for us. All the farms in our county will bring their best animals.

Each show animal has to be bathed and groomed. Along with washing each show pig, one of my chores is to clip off any long, unsightly hair from their ears, around their snouts, under their bellies and chins, and even along their tails. The pigs are tied to the wash rack with a rope in their mouths so they'll hold still long enough for me to trim the hair with electric clippers. They squeal and moan loudly from being tied, which makes the whole clipping process difficult and unpleasant.

Rusti doesn't have to be tied though. She just lets me clip her. In fact, she sits back on her haunches and nearly falls asleep. To get the lambs ready to show, we bathe them and then shear off their wool. We can't wait for other farmers to see this new crop of pigs we've raised. Expectations are high for our lambs as well. Wait until people see what a fine animal Rusti is!

Another chore for me is to go through our big show box and make sure we have enough brushes, medications, and any other supplies we'll need while we're at the show.

Penny gets her 4-H canning projects ready to take—canned fruits and vegetables, jellies, and preserves. She also has a dress and suit she's made that she'll enter in the fair. Mom has some canning of her own and a quilt she made to enter in the adult division.

The night before the stock show, we load supplies into Dad's truck and in the neck of our big stock trailer. It's hard work, but nobody minds. We're all excited about the show. When I finally drift off to sleep that night, I dream about Rusti winning grand champion of the show.

The next morning, we feed all the animals the same as always, including Rusti. Then Dad backs the truck up to our stock trailer, and I hitch it to the gooseneck hitch. After the animals finish eating, we load them into the trailer.

When we pull into the stock show, the first thing we do is unload all the animals. There are various sizes of pens. Some will fit four animals or more, and some will fit only one or two. Dad puts Rusti in a pen by herself. Next, we unload all the feed and supplies and situate them in a tack room near our pens.

After we finish getting everything put away and the animals bedded down, I take a quick walk around the show grounds. I love the smells, sights, and sounds of the stock show. Right now, the animal barns have a pleasant odor of fresh straw and wood shavings with just a hint of manure. As the show goes on, the manure odor will increase. It doesn't bother me though. I think this is how the world is supposed to smell.

All the animals have been taken away from their pens on farms around the county and put in unfamiliar pens here at the stock show. As I walk from the pig barn to the sheep barn to the cattle barn, the animals are letting their owners know that they don't particularly like the new place. Pigs are squealing, lambs are bleating, and cattle are bawling their displeasure.

As I walk through the barns, I greet friends I haven't seen for months, some for almost a full year. One of the exciting things about going to the livestock show is catching up with people I've missed and seeing how much they've changed.

In the cattle barn, I take a quick look around for Hannah, a girl I always enjoy seeing at the stock shows. I'm disappointed to see the place where she and her family will tie their steers is empty. They haven't made it to the show yet. She goes to school in a different town than I do, so we only see each other at stock shows and county 4-H events, maybe three or four times a year. She's really pretty and fun to be with, and her smile always makes me feel happy. Guess she's kind of my girlfriend. I can't wait for her to get here.

I head out to the midway and carnival. I pass a vendor making cotton candy and get a deep whiff of the sugary-sweet smell. In the carnival area, I'm greeted by the screams and laughter of kids on the rides. The rides clang and bump their way through a brief thrill for the riders. There's a mixture of old-time, calliope-sounding carnival music and more modern music being broadcast over loudspeakers around the carnival.

Carnies try to lure people over to participate in their games. They want you to spend way too much money trying to win a cheap stuffed toy. Dad says only suckers play the games at the carnival because they're rigged so you almost never win. As I pass another food stand, I breathe in the scents of popcorn, corn dogs, and funnel cakes. Another stand has bright red candy apples and yummy-looking caramel apples ready to be eaten. I buy a soda at one of the food booths and then head back to the pig barn to see what's happening there.

As I enter the barn, I notice farmers gathered around our pens. This is a sort of stock show ritual. Later on, Dad and I will walk around and see what other people have brought to the show. The farmers gravitate to Rusti's pen. Soon, a small crowd gathers around her pen. Rusti doesn't mind the attention. She stands there grunting and wringing her tail at the farmers as if to say, "Yes, look at me!"

"Tell you what," one of the farmers says to Dad. "You don't even have to take this gilt into the show ring. I'll take her off your hands just as she stands. How much you want for her?"

"This one's not for sale," Dad responds. "She's just for lookin'. I'll be glad to sell you one of her littermates or a half-sister if you wanna look at them."

Whew! That was close. I know Dad said we aren't selling Rusti, but she's drawing such a big crowd that I'm beginning to get a little worried.

"Sure you can't be talked out of her?" another farmer asks. "I can sure use one like her. She'd raise some awfully good show pigs over at my place. Maybe we can do some tradin' if you don't wanna sell her outright."

This farmer's offer is a much bigger challenge for Dad than the first man's. Dad's a part-time farmer who works a full-time job and farms on the side. He enjoys the farm life, like I do, and it's the way he and my mom want us kids to be

raised. This other man is a full-time farmer with a farm much bigger than ours. He's very successful and well respected, having built up a great reputation across the state and even nationwide. For him to take an interest in a pig we've raised would be a huge boost to our farm's reputation.

"You'll have to take it up with Cody," Dad says with a wink. "He's the one who hand-raised that gilt."

"That right, Cody?" asks the farmer. "You raised this gilt? Wait a minute. Is this the pig I've heard about? The one that thinks it's a dog, barks and wags its tail at the school bus?"

"Yes, sir. She's the one," I respond with pride. "Fact is, your daughter took up for Rusti when the older kids on the bus were bein' mean and makin' fun of her."

The farmer gives a big belly laugh. "So this is Rusti? Well, she's a well-known celebrity. Now I know I've gotta have her."

Other farmers listening in on the conversation laugh and nod in agreement. Apparently, Rusti's reputation is more widely known than I ever imagined. "Far as Duroc gilts go, she's 'bout as close to perfect as I've seen in a long time. In fact, 'bout the only flaw I can find is that faint scar on her left ham, but it doesn't amount to much."

"Tell you what I'll do," he continues. "If you sell her to me, I'll pay double what I'd normally pay for a gilt her age. Take my word for it, that's a pretty good offer. Might wanna think it over."

The offer brings whistles and murmurings from the other farmers. He didn't say exactly how much he's offering, but he's gotten everybody's attention by offering twice what a gilt her age is usually worth.

I glance over at Dad to see his reaction. He's beaming with pride—maybe the biggest smile I've ever seen on him. The only help he offers me is an open-hands gesture in my direction, telling me it's all up to me.

"I know that's a generous offer," I tell the farmer. "But no, thank you. We're gonna take Rusti home and let her raise some pigs on our farm. I'd sure like to show you some of her littermates and half-sisters though."

"Your dad's taught you well," the farmer says, laughing, as he slaps Dad on the back. "Let's go take a look at some of those littermates and half-sisters."

"Oh, and 'bout that scar," I continue. "It happened when a coyote just about got her as a little pig."

"No kiddin'?" the farmer responds. "I've had coyotes get after pigs at my place over the years. Mine usually got a lot worse than a little scar on one ham. How'd you get the coyote off her?"

"I didn't," I say. "Our dogs rescued her. They really got after that coyote. I don't think it'll be back to try its luck 'round our place any time soon."

"Wow, that's amazing," the farmer shoots back. "You must have some good dogs. After we look at these pigs, I might wanna talk to you 'bout where you got your dogs. My ol' dogs don't protect nothin'."

We both get a big laugh out of this.

Chapter Thirty

Friends for Life

Later, I return to the cattle barn and see that Hannah and her family have just pulled in. I pitch in to help unload their trailer and get their steers bedded down. Her dad appreciates my help, but I don't think it's much of a secret why I'm so willing. Hannah and I work side by side the whole time. We talk about what's been going on since we last saw each other, about school and our families.

"Wait 'til I tell you about Rusti," I tell her. "The dogs and I have had some awesome times with her over the summer."

"She the pig you rescued when she was a baby?" she asks. "I've heard about her. I hear she has a funny way of greetin' the bus when y'all get home from school."

We both laugh when I find out she's heard of

Rusti all the way over where she lives. We laugh a lot when we're together. Stories about Rusti, Bobo, Sancho, Simon, and me occupy much of our conversation as we work.

"You wanna meet Rusti?" I ask her when we're finished getting her steers and supplies settled.

We walk over to the pig barn, where Rusti greets Hannah with her typical charm, cute grunts, and tail wagging. Another person is added to the Rusti Fan Club. I show Hannah how to scratch behind her ears and on her belly.

"I can't believe how adorable she is," Hannah says. "Look at that cute nose and those long eyelashes. She's just perfect. The way she acts when I say somethin' to her, it seems like she'll start talkin' back to me any minute."

How cool is it that Rusti and Hannah have hit it off so well?

"Wait right here," Hannah says suddenly. "I'll be right back."

"Where're you goin'?"

"Just wait," she replies. "Be back in a minute."

I watch her head toward the cattle barn, scratching my head trying to figure out what made her take off like that. Almost as quickly as she left, she reappears with a large chunk of watermelon in her hand. The juice is already starting to drip through her fingers.

"Can Rusti have watermelon?" she asks. "Mom packed us some this mornin' before we left to come here."

I smile. "Are you kiddin'? It's only 'bout her favorite thing on earth."

She climbs into the pen with Rusti and feeds her the watermelon, not by putting it in her trough but by breaking off pieces and feeding it to her by hand.

"Oh, now you did it," I kid Hannah. "You have a friend for life. And you probably shot up to the top of her list of friends. She doesn't even get hand-fed watermelon by me."

In her sassy voice Hannah answers, "Well, us girls have to stick together, don't we?" Then she scratches Rusti behind her ears.

Now I have another good reason to like this girl. It's going to be a *great* stock show.

"Cody, I'm real proud of how you handled yourself today," Dad says later, as we're feeding the show animals before we get ready to go home. "Most grown men would've been swayed by that great offer for Rusti. You showed a lotta poise and confidence, and you were polite and respectful. Those are excellent qualities in a man."

Hearing my dad tell me he's proud of me, I think my heart might burst. "Think I might need to stay here tonight?" I ask Dad. "I'd be okay sleepin' on a bed of straw in the tack room. Wouldn't want anything to happen to our animals while we're not here." Rusti's squealing and grunting to let me know she doesn't like being at the stock show as much as she likes being in the yard with Bobo, Sancho, and Simon.

"I'm sure Rusti'll be fine," Dad responds, laughing. He knows the animal I'm most concerned about. "I'll need your help with the animals at home this evenin' and before we come up here in the mornin'. Besides, who else could I get to milk the cow?"

Reluctantly I agree, and we drive home to do our evening chores.

Chapter Thirty-one

Gone!

"Dad, Rusti's gone!" I cry out.

The first thing I did when we got to the stock show early that morning was go to Rusti's pen to check on her. But she wasn't there.

"What do you mean *gone*?" Dad says.

"I mean *gone*. The gate to her pen's open and she's not here," I moan. "Where on earth can she be?"

"Cody, are you sure her gate was latched when we left last night?" Dad arrives at her pen. "She comes and goes whenever she wants at home. If her gate wasn't latched, she might have pushed it open and gotten out. She wouldn't know to stay around like she does in the yard at home, so she could be just about anywhere."

"I'm positive I latched her gate," I respond. "It's the last thing I checked before we went home." Tears are welling up in my eyes, both from being heartbroken that Rusti's missing and from Dad thinking I might be to blame.

"Hey, Cody. Why'd you change your mind 'bout Rusti?" The question comes from the farmer who tried so hard to talk me out of her yesterday.

"He didn't change his mind," says Dad. "Know anything 'bout her bein' gone?"

"Well, I guess so," the farmer responds after he thinks it over. "I had a meeting early this mornin'. Thought it might last a while, so I got here early to feed. I saw two men takin' Rusti out of her pen. I figured someone must've made you a better offer than mine. You tellin' me you didn't sell her?"

"Did you recognize the two men?" Dad asks.

"Never seen 'em before," the farmer comes back. "I can tell you they don't know anything 'bout handlin' pigs. They started out pullin' on Rusti's ears and tail to try to get her to come with 'em. When they stopped tryin' to force her, she was okay to just follow 'em, kinda like a dog would."

Dad looks worried now. "Did you see where they took her?"

"Last I saw, they were headed out to where the trailers are parked. Might want to check and see if she's out there somewhere," the farmer responds. "You don't reckon those guys stole Rusti, do you? Just can't imagine it. Never even heard of someone stealin' a pig from a show. Let me know if there's anything I can do to help."

"Guess we'll have to find out what's going on," Dad replies. He takes out his cell phone and dials, and when he starts to talk, I can tell he's talking to the county sheriff's office.

"Cody, I need to tell you I'm sorry for doubtin' you earlier," he says as we wait for the sheriff's office to respond. "It's hard to think that someone might take a pig or any other animal from a stock show. I know how careful you are, so I shouldn't have jumped to the conclusion that you didn't latch her gate. I really am sorry."

"It's okay, Dad," I respond. "I sorta started doubtin' myself."

The sheriff's office stations a deputy at the show grounds during the stock show, so it doesn't take long for him to show up. He starts out by questioning Dad, me, and the farmer who saw Rusti being taken. He also questions other people with nearby pens. In no time, the whole stock show is buzzing about Rusti's "pig-napping."

After the deputy finishes talking to me, I grab a flashlight and head out to where the trailers are parked. As I shine my light into the trailers, I call Rusti's name, hoping that she'll squeal or grunt when she hears my voice. Having been to so many stock shows over the years, I recognize just about all the trailers. Like Dad and the farmer had said, it's hard to imagine that any of the farmers we know so well would steal a prized pig.

The sound of rustling in one of the trailers stops me in my tracks. Maybe it's her. My heart pounds in my chest as my hopes soar. "Rusti," I call out. I step up on the fender of the trailer, grab a side rail, and shine my flashlight inside.

BAM! Something slams into the side of the trailer from inside right next to my head, followed by loud and vicious barking. The force propels me backward off the fender and onto the ground, landing me on my feet, behind, back, and head. I

only got a brief look with my flashlight, but it was enough to know it was a huge dog with an angry red mouth and giant fangs. It can't get out of the trailer to get to me, but it still scared me all the way down to my toenails.

"*Phew.* Sure wasn't expectin' that," I murmur while trying to collect myself. Still shaking, I get back to my feet, dust myself off, and make sure all my parts work. Tears are rolling down my cheeks, partly from the fright I just experienced and partly from having my hopes so brutally dashed. Keeping in mind the sudden, jarring lesson I've just learned, I cautiously continue my search of the trailers.

Unfortunately, my search doesn't turn up anything else. If Rusti's in one of the trailers, she's not able to respond when I call her name. One thing I did notice is that Mr. Johnson's trailer isn't here. He has a farm not too far from our place. Sometimes, a farmer will pull his stock trailer home during a show if he needs it there, so it's not too unusual, but I make a mental note of it anyway.

The stock show goes on, and our other pigs

and the lambs win quite a few prizes. We send some pigs and lambs through the youth livestock auction and get really good prices per pound of body weight for them. When we sell our animals at the stock show, we use some of the money for the next year's animals, but most of it goes into a college fund for Penny, Clay, and me. The farmer who so badly wanted to buy Rusti purchases another gilt from her litter for a very nice price.

Under any other circumstances, this would be a very successful stock show for my family and a great reason for celebration. But Rusti's disappearance casts a gloomy cloud over everything. Hannah comes around now and then to try to comfort and encourage me. I appreciate her thoughtfulness, but even being around her doesn't ease the pain of losing Rusti.

As we pack up to take everything home, I'm fighting back tears. How can it be that Rusti's gone? I keep hoping I'll wake up from a bad dream. But it isn't a dream.

"Dad, are we really gonna go home without Rusti?" I ask as we're loading the other animals in our trailer. "Seems like the sheriff would've found something out by now."

"I know, son," Dad responds. "I hate to leave without her as much as you do. I'm sure the sheriff's doin' all he can. He just doesn't have much to go on."

When we get home from the stock show, I try to act like things are back to normal. But they aren't normal. It's just not the same without Rusti being here in the yard with Bobo, Sancho, and Simon. Everywhere I look I'm reminded of her. The dogs sense something's wrong as they search around for her. They miss their friend, too. They've lost some of the bounce in their step, and they don't wag their tails and jump around like before.

It's hard to believe she isn't here. It's three weeks until the next stock show, and I wish it were next week. That might distract me from thinking about her—maybe.

Chapter Thirty-two

Detectives on the Case

Something's been nagging at me since the day Rusti disappeared: Mr. Johnson's stock trailer that I expected to find at the stock show, but it wasn't there. His farm is only about four miles from our place. Even though we're neighbors, I don't really know Mr. Johnson or his sons. They're two of the kids on the school bus who were mean to Rusti and called her names. I know Mr. Johnson was at the stock show because I saw him standing toward the back of the crowd around Rusti's pen, listening to all that was being said.

Dad's not the kind of person to say anything bad about anybody. He believes if you can't say something nice, you better not say anything at all. About as close as I've heard him say something bad about someone is when he was talking about Mr. Johnson once and said, "He's a good man and a good farmer. Wish he didn't try to cut corners. When you start cuttin' corners, sooner or later it'll come back to bite you." I'm not sure what he meant by "cuttin' corners," but I think it means trying to find the fast and easy way to do things. Dad's always taught me that hard work and patience always pay off.

"Hey, guys. Wanna see if we can find Rusti?" I say to the dogs early in the morning after three days of moping around.

Just the sound of her name perks them up. After I finish my morning chores, Bobo, Sancho, and I set out. We're going to check out Mr. Johnson's farm.

My head is filled with all kinds of questions and emotions as we make the four-mile walk to the Johnson's farm. *What if Rusti's not there at all? What if it was just a coincidence that Mr. Johnson's trailer wasn't parked with the other trailers at the stock show? But, what if she is there? Or, was there? What if something terrible has happened to her? What if Mr. Johnson has done something to hurt her? How will I even be able to try to find Rusti if*

Mr. Johnson or even his wife and boys are there? They might not want to let me take a look around. The thought of having my hopes of finding her being dashed again makes the walk to the neighbor's farm another gut-wrenching experience in the Rusti pig-napping saga.

Like Dad, Mr. Johnson's a part-time farmer. By the time the dogs and I make the walk to his farm, he's gone to work—thank goodness. Their car's also gone, so I'm thinking his wife and boys might not be home either. They have a dog, but it's tied up on a chain. No one comes out of the house when it barks, which confirms my belief that they're all gone.

Mr. Johnson doesn't try to keep up with his farm like Dad does, so things look kind of rundown. The paint on the barns is weathered and peeling. Several wood fences have rails that are busted, and it looks like they've been that way for a while. One positive thing I notice is that he doesn't have as big a problem with pig weed and thistles as we do.

Bobo and Sancho go right past all the other pens and buildings and straight to a small barn.

It's all sealed up, with the door chained and padlocked. Sure looks like somebody might be trying to hide something. Bobo whines and paws at the door, while Sancho stands with his front paws on the wall of the barn, wagging his tail and yipping.

"Rusti, you in there?" I call out.

There's a squealing and grunting response from a pig in the barn. I don't know if I can tell one pig's sounds from another, but if I can, then I really think the sounds I'm hearing are coming from Rusti. Sancho finds a small gap under one of the boards of the barn and squeezes under it. Soon, I hear him making happy whining sounds and a pig responding. Now I'm even more convinced we've found Rusti. As much as we hate to, the dogs and I have to leave her there until we can come back with Dad. The four-mile walk home seems much shorter, knowing we've found our friend.

"Dad, we've found Rusti," I tell Dad as soon as he gets home from work. I tell him about the missing trailer at the stock show on the day Rusti disappeared and how the dogs and I went to the Johnson's farm and found a pig locked up in a barn.

"Son, you know that's trespassin'," Dad says. "You can't go snoopin' around another farm without permission. You can be arrested for that. Now what makes you think the pig is Rusti? Did you see her?"

"No, sir," I answer. "The door on the barn has a chain and padlock. There aren't any windows, so there wasn't any way to see in. But she squealed at me when I called her name, like she always does here, and the dogs got really excited 'bout findin' her."

"That's not much to go on," Dad replies. "Not sure I'd even ask the sheriff to come take a look with no more than that."

"Dad, I'm sure it's her. Won't you trust me on this?" I plead.

Scratching his head and thinking it over a moment, Dad sighs. "All right, I'll call the sheriff. But this'll be the only time if you're wrong." He calls the sheriff, who's out of his office checking on some other things. Good for us he's not far away, so he tells Dad he'll meet us at the Johnson's farm in about fifteen minutes.

Dad and I put Bobo and Sancho in the truck

with us to go to Mr. Johnson's farm. He's doing evening chores when we come up his drive following the sheriff's car. Bobo and Sancho jump out of the truck as soon as we stop and run up to the same padlocked barn, wagging their tails and yipping.

"That the barn?" Dad asks.

"Yes, sir," I reply. "Can you hear her squealin' and gruntin' at the dogs?"

"We'd like to take a look inside that barn," the sheriff tells Mr. Johnson.

He scowls. "You got a search warrant, Sheriff?"

"No, but you know I can get one if I need to," says the sheriff.

"Naw, that's all right. I'll let you look in my barn. Got nothin' to hide."

Mr. Johnson unlocks the door. With the limited light from the open door we can see a gilt there in a pen. She's a red pig all right, but this one has black spots. It looks exactly like Rusti, but it can't be her. Rusti doesn't have any black markings at all.

My heart sinks, and I feel lower than a snake's belly in a wagon rut. I've dragged Dad and the

sheriff over here for nothing. Worst thing is the dogs and I didn't find our friend after all.

The dogs go over to the pen and touch noses with the pig. They whine and wag their tails, and the pig grunts and wrings her tail just like Rusti. Now I'm confused. How many other pigs can there be that act like this?

"Satisfied?" asks Mr. Johnson with a smirk.

"Sheriff, I'd like to take the pig out into the light," says Dad. "I wanna see if she has a scar on her left ham."

"You ain't takin' my pig anywhere," Mr. Johnson responds. He steps forward and gets right in Dad's face, toe to toe.

Dad doesn't back down, holding his ground and staring right back in Mr. Johnson's eyes.

While Dad has Mr. Johnson distracted, I slip over to the pen and run my hand down the side of the pig. The hair where the black spots are feels different from the red. It's kind of rough and sticky.

"Hey, kid. Stay away from my pig," Mr. Johnson scolds. "In fact, you can all get outta my barn and off my place."

"Dad, look!" I exclaim. I show him my hand. Something black has rubbed off the pig.

"What's that?" the sheriff asks.

I rub my fingers together and smell my hand. "I think it might be shoe polish."

"Cody, bring the pig out in the light," the sheriff instructs.

I open the gate of the pen. The pig comes over to the dogs and me, squealing and rooting playfully on me. She then walks out of the barn with us. We all look at her left ham, and, sure enough, she has that familiar scar.

It IS Rusti! **We've found her!**

I'm so excited I can hardly breathe. Finding a faucet, I take my shirt off and start to scrub her to get the shoe polish spots off. Mom'll fuss at me for ruining my shirt, but right now I don't care.

The sheriff arrests Mr. Johnson, puts handcuffs on him, and makes him sit in the back seat of the patrol car. His wife and sons are watching, with her wiping tears from her cheeks and the boys staring in stunned disbelief. I feel sorry for them. It kind of puts a damper on the excitement of finding Rusti. Mr. Johnson sits in the patrol car with his head down, unwilling to even make eye contact with his family.

Dad loads the dogs in the truck and drives back to our farm. The sheriff and I wait with Rusti, while Dad returns with a trailer. When we get her loaded into it, we're ready to take Rusti home. The sheriff tells us we can come in tomorrow and file charges. He then takes Mr. Johnson to the county jail.

When we get home, I let Rusti out in the yard with Bobo, Sancho, and Simon. The dogs are as excited as I've ever seen them. They're thrilled to have their friend back home, and even Simon purrs and rubs on Rusti in an unusual show of affection. I call Hannah to tell her we've found her, and she's almost as excited as me. Now life can truly get back to normal.

Later, Dad gets a phone call from Mr. Johnson's wife. It's obvious that she's upset because Dad tells her several times to relax and take a deep breath. He ends the conversation by saying, "We'll see what we can do."

Chapter Thirty-three

Doin' Right

The next morning, after we finish our chores, Dad doesn't go to work like usual. Instead, he tells me we have business in town that we need to take care of.

"Can I go too?" Clay asks as Dad and I come back into the kitchen after we've changed out of our work clothes.

"No, son," responds Dad. "This is something Cody and I have to do."

Clay stands by the door, pouting.

We don't even eat breakfast with the rest of the family. Mom knows what we're about. She's already made us each a breakfast sandwich with scrambled eggs, sausage, and cheese, and wrapped them in paper towels. As we walk out the door, she hands us our sandwiches along with travel cups—coffee for Dad and milk for me.

On the porch, Mom gives Dad a kiss and a hug then does the same for me. "I love you. I'll be praying for you both," she says as we start toward the truck.

Penny pats me on the shoulder. "Good luck."

Dad and I get in his truck to drive to the county jail. "Your mom's sure a good cook, isn't she?" he says as we eat our breakfast sandwiches.

"Yep," I reply. "She sure takes good care of us."

We don't say very much else on the way. I guess we're both deep in thought about what we have to do.

When we get to the county jail, Dad asks the jailer if we can talk to Mr. Johnson. The jailer brings him into a room with Dad and me.

Before Dad has a chance to say anything, Mr. Johnson says, "I'm so sorry for what I did. It was just wrong. I heard all the other farmers talkin' about that gilt at the stock show, heard how much that one man was willin' to pay for her. I know I could never spend even half that much to get a pig like her. I'm not tryin' to make excuses. There aren't any excuses for what I've done. I'm just tryin' to tell you what I was thinkin'. I know it was wrong thinkin'." He looks at me. "Cody, I know you raised that gilt from a little pig. I'm really sorry for what I did to you. I know I deserve to spend time in jail for takin' her. I want you both to know how truly sorry I am."

"Who were the guys who took her out of her pen?" Dad asks.

"They were just some guys from another county who I hired for day labor," Mr. Johnson responds. "They didn't know what was goin' on. If the gilt hadn't been so trustin' of people, those two would never have gotten her to the trailer. All the blame for what's happened is on me." He shakes his head, obviously disgusted with himself.

Dad tells him he wants to talk to me alone, and we go out of the room into the hall. "Cody, will you be willin' to drop the charges?" he asks.

"Dad, are you serious? He stole Rusti. Is it right for him to get off scot-free?"

"I know what he did, son," Dad replies. "It was wrong, and I believe it when he says he knows it. There are times when we all do things we know are wrong, things we wish we could take back. I'd like to give him a second chance. Isn't that how you'd like to be treated? When Mrs. Johnson called last night, she said they might lose their farm if he has to spend time in jail. I don't want that. Do you?"

I sure don't. "No, sir. I felt real bad for Mrs. Johnson and boys when the sheriff arrested him."

Dad continued, "Sometimes the easiest thing to do when someone wrongs you is to try to get back at 'em and punish 'em. The harder thing to do is forgive 'em and help 'em work through it. I'd like for us to do the harder thing if that's okay with you."

"I guess I'm okay with droppin' the charges," I finally say.

When Dad and I go back into the room with Mr. Johnson, Dad says, "Cody and I have decided to drop the charges."

Mr. Johnson looks like he can't believe it. His jaw drops open and tears well up in his eyes.

Dad continues, "If you'll let me, I'd like to help you work on upgradin' your herd. Maybe we can work together to improve both our farms. I'd sure like for us to be closer as neighbors and friends."

"You'd really do that for me after all I've put you through?" Mr. Johnson asks in shock. "I don't know what to say. I know how well you run your farm. I'd love it if mine ran half that good. If you're willin' to do that for me, I'm sure willin' to try."

"C'mon. We'll give you a ride home," Dad offers. "We'll talk on the way 'bout how we can work together."

As we drive, Dad and Mr. Johnson talk about different things they might do. At first Mr. Johnson doesn't say much. When he does speak, he sounds pretty sad. Then Dad says something about the problem we have on our farm with pig weed and thistles and asks how he thinks we might better control them.

Mr. Johnson's mood suddenly changes. He tells Dad about an herbicide that does a number on pig weed and thistles but doesn't hurt the grass and is safe for livestock. The more questions Dad asks, the more Mr. Johnson perks up. By the time we get to his farm, Dad and he are talking about their operations and making plans for improvements, just like good friends and neighbors.

The Johnsons' dog barks at us when we drive

up the driveway, bringing Mrs. Johnson and the boys out of the house. As soon as he sees his family, Mr. Johnson can't hold back anymore. Tears roll down his face. He shakes Dad's hand and then mine, but he's too choked up to speak.

Dad simply says, "Have a good afternoon, my friend."

Mrs. Johnson runs up to our truck as he gets out and gives him a huge hug. While they're hugging, I can see tears running down her cheeks. She looks at Dad and mouths the words, "Thank you."

Dad smiles and gives her a little salute, then we drive away.

Dad and I don't say anything on our way to our place. I guess we're both savoring the moment. It's hard for me to imagine that Dad has ever done anything wrong. What he did today wasn't wrong. In fact, it couldn't have been more right. He really is a good man. I hope that I can be half the man Dad is.

Chapter Thirty-four

Return to the Barns

We don't take Rusti to any other stock shows. Once was enough. Besides, she received more notoriety from that one show than most pigs would receive by winning the top prize at ten shows. We're content to keep her in the safety of our farm with Bobo, Sancho, and Simon.

"It's time for Rusti to return to the barns to do what she's meant to do," Dad tells me one day. "We need her to become a mama sow and have baby show pigs."

Dad's right. But taking her back to the barns isn't going to be easy for me to do, especially after all we've been through together. A new school year is about to begin, and between getting the pigs and lambs ready for the stock shows and going to school, I won't have much time to spend with Rusti anyway. Still, I'm torn about taking her back to the barns to live permanently.

Rusti's gotten back into the routine of living in the yard with Bobo, Sancho, and Simon. I've looked forward to finding her at the back door every morning. I know I'm going to miss having her around the yard, and I'm certain Bobo and Sancho are going to miss her as well. Even Simon will miss her in his own snooty way.

Bobo, Sancho, Simon, and I reluctantly go with Rusti for her return to the barns. She doesn't seem to mind being put in the pen with other soon-to-be-mothers her age. You'd think she almost understands that's where she needs to be. I'm glad the gilts got to know each other over the summer, when Rusti came with me to do my chores and during the time they spent together at the stock show.

She lies down with the other gilts under the shed instead of with Bobo and Sancho in the yard. She learns to eat at the big troughs when Dad feeds them. She doesn't even try to escape and return to the yard the way she did when she was young.

I guess there are changes we all face as we grow up and begin new phases of our lives. Rusti appears to be willing to accept and embrace the next part of her life. Too bad the rest of us are having such a hard time adjusting to life without our friend in the yard.

Chapter Thirty-five

Full Circle

A few months later, it's time for Rusti's first litter of pigs to be born. Most of the time when I take a sow to the farrowing house, I have to drive her or try to lure her there with feed. With Rusti, I only have to open the gate of her pen and let her out. The two of us walk together to the wash rack and farrowing house.

"You probably don't remember it, but this is the same farrowin' house where you were born," I tell her. "This time I'll help you have your babies."

Unlike her mother, Rusti isn't grouchy with me for being in the farrowing house with her. She knows I'm not here to hurt her or her babies and doesn't chase me out of the pen. Bobo, Sancho, and Simon are right outside the house keeping an eye on us.

As I dry each of Rusti's eight babies and help them learn to nurse, memories of her growing up flood back to me: when she was such a pretty little red gilt, how she played in the yard with Bobo and Sancho, her amazing curiosity, the time when the coyote attacked, how she joined the dogs in welcoming the school bus home each afternoon, even the harrowing time of her being pig-napped.

All of Rusti's babies are nursing now. She's grunting rhythmically as they nurse, singing her own motherly lullaby to them. As I look at her babies, I smile and wonder about them. *Will some of them want to nuzzle with me? Will they want me to rub behind their ears and under their bellies? Will they try to catch watermelon clods? Which ones might be champions in the show ring?*

I already have my eye on a little boar that's bigger and more developed than the other pigs in the litter. Two pretty little gilts have also caught my attention and appear to have a lot of potential. *Could these pigs from Rusti's first litter be prize show pigs in six months?*

Looking back, I can't help but think about how different it would have been if we had put Rusti down instead of hand-raising her to be the fine animal she's become. It would have been acceptable if we had put her down to save all the other pigs in her litter, but I'm so glad we didn't.

I'm thankful Dad was willing to give me a chance to raise Rusti. It allowed her to become a friend to Bobo, Sancho, Simon, and me, and now she's becoming a great mama sow. I'm privileged to get to see her babies grow into what might be fine show pigs. Thank goodness we made the decision to save her. It was the right thing to do.

Knowing how much Rusti likes it, I reach down and scratch her behind her ears. "Rusti, I can't wait for the adventure that awaits your babies. If they're anything like you, it'll be so much fun!"

She looks at me with those pretty dark eyes and grunts as if she understands. Then she closes her eyes for a well-deserved nap.

Glossary

Boar – a domestic male pig that has not been neutered.

Breeding stock – animals used for raising livestock for market or show.

Duroc – a pig of a reddish breed developed in North America.

Farrow – a sow giving birth to baby pigs.

Farrowed – baby pigs being born.

Farrowing house – a place where a domestic sow gives birth to pigs.

Gilt – a young female pig that has not yet farrowed, or given birth to pigs.

Guidance counselor – a person who is employed, usually in a school, to offer advice on problems and assist students in making career or college plans.

Jersey – dairy cattle originating from Jersey in England.

Livestock show or stock show – an event where farm and ranch animals are exhibited and judged.

Marauder – a person or animal that goes from one place to another looking for people to attack.

Rhode Island Red – a bird of an American breed of reddish-black, domestic chicken.

Social graces – skills used to interact politely in social situations, including manners, etiquette, deportment, and fashion.

Sow – an adult female pig, especially one that has farrowed or given birth to pigs.

Southdown – a celebrated breed of short-wooled, hornless sheep.

Steer – a male, domestic, bovine animal that has been neutered and is raised for beef.

Tortoise – a turtle, typically an herbivorous one that lives on land.

Wean – to get a child or young animal accustomed to taking food other than milk.

About the Author

PHILIP PEARCE grew up on his family's farm in New Mexico, raising and exhibiting 4-H pig and lamb projects with his siblings. After high school, he moved to Texas to attend Texas A&M University where he earned a degree in Agricultural Economics and an MBA in Finance. Philip has lived more than forty years as a paraplegic wheelchair user after a fall from an oil service derrick as a college student rendered him paralyzed, but his disability has never dampened his zest for life or his spirit of endurance.

Today, Philip shares some of his experiences through writing and visiting with young people about challenges they may face in their own lives. He lives in Texas with his wife Karen where he is Gramps to four grandkids.

Made in the USA
Middletown, DE
09 October 2020